CATS DON'T CARE FOR MONEY

Books by Christiane Rochefort

WARRIOR'S REST

CHILDREN OF HEAVEN

CATS DON'T CARE FOR MONEY

CHRISTIANE ROCHEFORT

CATS DON'T CARE FOR MONEY

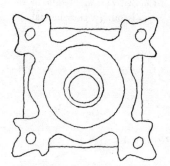

Translated from
the French by
HELEN EUSTIS

1965
DOUBLEDAY & COMPANY, INC., GARDEN CITY, NEW YORK

CATS DON'T CARE FOR MONEY

THE WHOLE PROBLEM is that girls like me aren't trained for it. We have no background for the whole business. We find a full-fledged, well-established, going concern, solid as a rock to all appearances, looking as if it's always been that way and always will be to the end of time, and there's no reason for it to change. It's how things are. Everyone says so, and, at first, you believe it. Why not, since you don't know any better? Oh, sometimes you begin to wonder, isn't it sort of—isn't it too—I mean, isn't it a bit much? but to see it for what it really is, just plain stupid, that takes time, and common sense. In the meantime you just have to put up with it. Especially with men, who are, you might say, our natural field of endeavor, and towards whom we react with indecision, weakness, and ambivalence, if not downright idiocy.

The truth is that as soon as you fall in love you ought to put in earplugs. But that's just the moment when you're in no condition to think of it.

Why don't you let your hair grow? asked Philippe—six feet one, blond, periwinkle eyes, adorable nose, willful mouth, broad and intelligent forehead, etc.—I'd like you so much better with long hair at least you'd look like a woman, why are you wearing slacks again when you know I like you better in a dress, if you love me said Philippe, can't you try to please me just in this little thing. And in that little thing. That shouldn't be such an effort if you really love me said Philippe, what time did you go to bed last night and, if I may ask, what were you up to when you got there, in my opinion you're wasting your time with all those books when you don't remember a word you read anyway. And you still haven't sewed that missing button on your jacket, don't look so surprised, I told you about it last week and I can see it's the same jacket. And with me, the man who only goes out with girls who are impeccably groomed, dressed to the teeth! Me, who would love so much to show you off! I'm telling you all this for your own sake you know, if I didn't care for you it wouldn't matter to me that your way of life can only lead to disaster, I'd be satisfied to have the same kind of good time with you that most men have with girls who are more or less "free" like you, they're only too happy for you all to remain "free," yes indeed! for them it's not only practical, it's economical, you must know what I mean, you with all your experience. But it just so happens that my interest in you is different, so I try to help you, said Philippe, but you have to make an effort too—hold your fork in the other hand, don't laugh like that it's vulgar, don't roll your bread up that way, it's dirty, stand up straight you smoke too much you're staining your teeth don't drink so much it's not nice for a woman, you don't look too well you should see a doctor. Why don't you look for a regular job instead of doing a lot of odd ones that get you nowhere, honestly your carelessness upsets me, what's going to become of you, you'll ruin your health with all that coffee. Promise me that tomorrow you'll go to bed at midnight, just to please me, said Philippe, if you don't do it for yourself at least do it for me, I wonder what you think you're doing with that bunch of misfits, what do you see in them? They aren't for you, you deserve better than that, if you want to make me happy you'll stop seeing them . . . If you love me said Philippe, couldn't you do this, that would please me, and not that, which doesn't? It's not so difficult.

Thus spake Philippe, and me, I listened, openmouthed. I drank in his words. I found they made sense.

And anyway, where is this kind of life getting you? Hm? I mean, in the end, where is it getting you?

What could I answer? Nowhere, it's getting me nowhere. But then it isn't intended to get me anywhere, and anyway, get me where? Where is it meant to get me? Well, I don't know. You see, he said, smiling, you see perfectly well that you don't know.

The truth is I don't know anything any more. That man is an Attila. He leaves a desert in his wake. I walk around in a daze. Who am I? What are we doing here? It's a mystery. Oh, those great confused thoughts! he says. It sounds very fine, very poetic, but when you really take a look at them, it's Fogsville. Fogsville, he repeats, pleased with his phrase. Life, you know, life isn't like that, it's much simpler than that, baby. Don't you ever want to lead a normal life? said Philippe.

3

Normal. What's that? What is a normal life in the world we live in? I'm willing, but what is it?

But Philippe seemed to know. His air of assurance put my uncertainties to flight. Uncertainties are fragile. Since I've known Philippe I've been coming apart at the seams. I'm dissolving, I don't know where I'm going any more, I'm a dust mote in space, and in this state of confusion I have only one place of refuge: his arms. There everything is calm, serene, quiet, and warm. Peace is there, and security.

You see. You see, my little kitten. You need someone. You can't make it all alone. You act proud, but underneath you're just a tiny little girl who needs to be protected, like everybody else. There, there. You see. Doesn't it feel good in my arms?

Oh yes, it feels good! Oh yes. It feels good. That's the trouble. Philippe is strong, he's solid, he's sure. He knows.

He's here. He talks. And poor me I'm listening to him with my mouth hanging open, in a dress, with hair down to my shoulders and my fork in the correct hand. I went to the doctor, I swallowed yellow pills. I arrived on time, relying on the watch he'd given me just for that, which I set ahead so as to be extra sure. I loved him. Some nights I went to bed at midnight so that I could tell him about it the next day, feeling proud of myself and accepting praise from his mouth: That's a good girl, my little kitten, you must keep it up, you'll see how much better you'll feel. I did feel better. I loved him. I cleaned up my damned room when he was coming. He didn't like my room but since he lived in his family's apartment he had to come there to sleep with me. He tried to overlook what he still called my

4

mess, even after all the trouble I'd taken to clean it up; he tried not to see the stuff pinned on the walls, among it several rather indecent portraits of me by obviously different hands, plus some other battle souvenirs which I wasn't hypocrite enough to take down and which bothered him; he'd rather not have seen my bed, because its state of wear and tear seemed to him evidence of previous unmentionable activities, and he particularly hated the spread on which he assumed they had taken place, he found it in dreadful taste and after all the others who preceded him he put his beloved buttocks on it with all the fastidiousness of a virgin, until Christmas, when, on aesthetic grounds, and playing Santa Claus, he gave me a new one, one with no memories, on which he could feel more comfortable. He loved me. He wished me well. And nothing seemed less compatible with all the good things he wanted for me than my way of life, my surroundings, my friends, my habits, my clothes, my hair, my language, my tastes, my ideas, anything which wasn't my true self—that true self which was buried, stifled, hidden, which he loved because he was the only one who knew it, and which was destined to be brought to life by his hands like a pearl wrested from an oyster. . . . And I listened to him, my mouth hanging open, in a dress, with my hair down to the middle of my back. And no earplugs. And he had a lovely voice.

"Can you honestly say you're happy this way?"

He wasn't the first who had taken that kind of interest in me, I mean had been interested in that way I knew so well and mistrusted: an enlightened interest, a generous interest, in my life, my occupations, nay even in my thoughts, etc. I'd already had a few men in my room who had looked around, asked questions, what do you do, how do you live, on what, and then had sighed, Poor baby! Or Poor bunny! or kitten, or pussycat, according to their education or profession or the current style. Once I was even called My poor beastie—he got that out of a movie, a brand-new one. They always get it from somewhere. Then they stroke my face and hold me against their shoulder. They're going to Help me. To Protect me. From this wicked world where I've got lost. A poor lost baby (kitten, pussycat, beastie, etc.). They have a thing about young women in distress.

That kills me. I'm not in distress, at most a little broke, simply because I hate boring jobs and it's hard to find work that isn't boring, and frankly if they really were interested in my welfare it would be better after making their beautiful speeches to slip me a little dough in a friendly way, since they always say they're pals. But it's always just a question of moral support. Maybe I could get some cash finally, after working hard at letting myself be supported morally, at sobbing on their shoulders, in short playing the game according to the rules, patiently. It seems to me, though, that if you have to work all that hard, you might as well be a real whore—you make more and it's quick, or, since I really haven't the personality for it (too many inconveniences), go to an office. So I usually reassure them at once, I live this way because I like it. It's my style. Shelter, food, and clothing. Period. That way I don't have to put up with so much nonsense. It's my style. I'm not complaining.

6

All right. All right if you aren't complaining why should I. All right. The noble thoughts go back to their hope chest, the clear gaze of good will becomes opaque once more, a whole chemistry is set in motion. I don't know if I make myself clear but that doesn't matter. I'm used to it. Anyway it's quite mysterious: what really did happen? Somehow it seemed simple; and yet, it isn't. No. It's complicated. It's as if we weren't talking about the same thing. It seems that the world is one big game and one should play according to certain rules. So I ruined it. So what, to hell with it. There are always plenty of other men where these came from.

Or that's what I used to say. But I can't say to hell with Philippe. There aren't plenty of Philippes. There's only one, this one; only one who has these eyes these hands this voice, and this capacity to rouse me in just the right way which has made me forget that there used to be others who had the same.

And I call it Love.

"Come on, tell the truth, are you happy living this way?"

How can I answer that? Yes or no. Happy. What does it mean. Do I know? Happy? No, certainly not. So what?

"To hell with happiness!"

"Oh, come off it! You aren't all that different. Everybody wants to be happy."

"I say to hell with it."

"Being unhappy just to prove you're different is pushing originality a little far, don't you think?"

"But Philippe—that's not it. . . . I don't care whether

7

or not I'm like everybody else, that isn't it, but if everybody else happens to be a jerk . . ."

"There you go, waving your revolutionary banner. What are you reading these days, pussycat, Mao Tsetung?"

"*France-Dimanche!* Shit, they make me—"

"And a vocabulary to match!"

"—shit with all their happiness. The Shah is happy, the Princess is happy, the meat packer is happy, everybody's nuts on the subject. Yesterday I bought a pound of butter marked the Happiness Butter, no, I swear I'm not kidding! There are Happiness lamps, too, you're supposed to feel happy when they're lit. It's very fashionable. They all were happy and had many happy children. With the atomic bomb hanging over them. Waiting for it to fall. Shit."

"You and your bomb, you work it in everywhere."

"*I* work it in everywhere? *I* work it in? Oh shit! I suppose I invented it?"

"Oh come on, can't you say a sentence without using the word 'shit'? It gets monotonous."

"I can't help it that the subject makes it appropriate."

"What subject? I was talking to you about being happy, I can't see how that calls for such a word."

"I do. Shit on happiness."

"All right." He sighs. "In that case there's nothing left for me to do but leave. I don't know what I'm doing here. All I ever dream of is making you happy. I have only one thought: your happiness." He puts down the bread he's been crumbling; he looks away from me; the sun is veiled, the sky darkens. I have made a mistake. I have expressed myself. I shouldn't have. Why couldn't I have shut up? I don't know what happens to me every time. When you're in love you don't just need earplugs, you should plaster your mouth with adhesive tape.

"I really don't know why I take an interest in you. It's discouraging, you know. . . ."

Please God, do something! He's going to leave! Forever! And what shall I do then? What shall I do without him? The empty days, the nights . . .

"I'm getting discouraged . . . I'm wondering if I'm not wasting my time. While I." Sigh. "Look, Céline, I'm at a crucial point in a man's life. It's a point when he has to make Decisions. Serious decisions. And they're decisions which depend partly on you. And you! You . . ."

Ouch.

"You just don't understand anything, or if you do, it's worse really, because it means you don't give a damn what I do or don't do, or whether I'm here or not, I'm just one of the crowd . . ."

"Philippe . . ."

". . . that passes through your life. While I only dream about keeping you near me—always—"

Ouch, ouch, ouch, ouch. Oh my heart! Oh my weak knees! Oh that word! Why am I so soft, so melting, suddenly? What magic is there in that word? What poison?

". . . every day that's all I fight for. . . . Against my mother, against my father—who have other ideas about what I should do, believe me, and who never stop nagging me about them. The number of eligible girls my mother has thrown at my head . . . and whom I haven't even looked at . . . Don't you realize a decision like this is a sacrifice on my part? On top of all the rest do I have to fight with you too? I'm not going to keep on forever, you know. I'm warning you."

Ouch.

"If you don't want to be happy I can't very well force you to be. . . ."

Tralala. Happiness, with horns and a cloven hoof, peers at me round a turning of the road. In the middle of the road of our life. Temptation. Liberty or Love? The knife at the throat. In the name of what could I say no? In the name of Freedom. Freedom from what? Freedom from what? From what? You are twenty-seven, says Philippe, it's time you knew what you wanted of life. You're a little old for daydreams, says Philippe. It's time. It's time. Or you'll wake up too late and find you missed the boat. (What boat? What boat?)

"I see you don't answer. If that's all my words mean to you . . ."

I absolutely have to say something. Absolutely.

"Philippe . . ."

That's not quite enough. He doesn't think so either.

"Yes?"

"It's not that I don't want to be happy, that's not what I mean. . . ."

"Then what do you mean?"

"I mean . . . (lend me your comb, will you?) . . . that's not the idea . . . in life . . ."

"Oh? Then what is the idea? Answer me. —Eh?— What is the idea in life?"

"Hmm. I don't know."

"Just fine. Obviously if you don't know what—what it's all about it's really worth suffering for, all the days of your life. Sacrificing your happiness. It's a beautiful thing to suffer for one's ideas. What's the matter? But look Céline, what is it? but you're crying!"

What else can I do? Honestly, what else could I do? It's true, I don't know what it's all about! I'm in a complete fog, I don't understand anything.

"Look, baby . . ."

He smiles. My weakness strengthens him. He's happy. He takes my hand.

"You mustn't cry like that in front of everybody! People will think I'm a sadistic brute! . . . You don't think I'm trying to hurt you, do you? I'm only trying to put a little sense into your pretty head." He strokes the aforementioned. "It's full of wrong ideas, ideas that hurt you. Ideas that distort the way things really are. And I . . ."

He's holding my hand. Here come the oysters, he lets it go, to grab his plate.

". . . and you know that I," he swallows an oyster, "don't want to hurt you," another oyster, "uselessly." He swallows. "I want you to be happy." He swallows. "Even in spite of yourself." He swallows another oyster. "And you cry! Come on, eat, they're delicious!" He swallows. "You act as if I were trying to give you poison. Am I poison?" He swallows an oyster. He sighs. "The truth is you don't love me."

"Oh Philippe!"

He swallows two oysters.

"Well then? Why do you refuse to admit your feelings? Why so many principles? Principles of what? You don't even know yourself! Why do you try to hide everything that's best in you? I know what's best in you." He swallows an oyster.

"What is it?"

"You're a woman."

They're really wonderful.

I look at him. Suppose I were to say to him: I know what's best in you, it's that you are a man. Please, what would that mean? The best thing about you is that you are a man. Yes. The best thing about a banana is that it's a banana. Well, that's true enough. But a banana really is a banana. While a man—

"What are you thinking?"

"Nothing."

With experience comes wisdom. Adhesive tape. Since the danger has been averted, Philippe is still here, eating oysters as if he had no idea of moving from his chair, all I have to do is behave myself.

"Yes you are. I can see you thinking. I can always tell when you're thinking."

"I'm thinking about bananas."

"While you're eating oysters?"

"Actually the oysters are very good. The best thing about them is that they are oysters. I want some more."

"Won't it make you sick?"

"Oh come on, I have a cast-iron stomach!"

"That's what people always say and then they're sorry later."

"Pfui on later."

"Well! For once you didn't say shit!"

"See, I'm making progress!"

He laughs. He's happy. He orders more oysters.

"I'd like more wine, too."

"My God, have you already absorbed the whole bottle?"

"What do you mean, me! How about you?"

"You know I hardly touch white wine. On the other hand, you touch it a little too often, if I may say so . . . if you're planning on finishing another bottle before the Brouilly . . ."

"I don't want any Brouilly, I'll keep on with this. I hate to change wines during a meal."

"With coq au vin? You can't drink Sancerre with coq au vin!"

"Why not?"

"But look . . . one must drink red wine with coq au vin. . . . And anyway you drink too much. For a woman."

"What is a woman?"

"Aha, you keep coming back to it! It's what you don't want to be," he says humorously.

"Me?"

"Yes, you!"

He laughs. He's happy. He knows what he's talking about: one, what a woman is; two, that I don't want to be one. Me. I, who have spent these past months in his arms (not to mention those of all the others before him who shall be nameless)—I am Refusing my Destiny as Woman.

"It's true," he insists with a warm smile, "you don't want to be a woman."

The trouble is that since men have the use of speech they're always eager to use it; although it would be so much cagier to be still. Talking goes on without anybody's leave no matter when no matter how, and no matter what. On the other hand, what else can you do when nothing is happening? There are spaces to be filled. Words fill them. Even loving doesn't take up every moment of living, it seems; there's a certain emptiness in everything. So here I am, waiting for what comes next, and in the meantime asking him for a definition: what does he understand by the word "woman," because I certainly feel like one, in fact I'm quite pleased with myself. So I'd like to know what he . . . He has a definition. I should have known. It's like a nest of boxes. First of all, a woman is made for loving. Aha, now we must have a definition of Loving, there's another box, equally empty, containing another box, also empty.

"I've spent my life at that!" (The adhesive tape, girl, the adhesive tape! Too late.)

Not at all. Not what I was doing. What I was doing wasn't really loving. It has a very different name (I'd forgotten, with other people it's called getting laid) and besides I'd be better off forgetting about that, it's nothing to be proud of, and it isn't very pleasant for Him to hear about when He's doing his utmost to put the whole thing out of his mind out of consideration for me. And can I tell him what possible good I got out of all that?

"None."

"You see. Where did it get you?"

"Well, since it came to nothing it needn't worry you."

"There you go, arguing again."

14

Me arguing.

"What do you call it when you do it?"

"I talk seriously," he says. "At least I try. And I deserve some credit for it, because it isn't so easy with you."

"Because I answer when you talk?"

"You see. There you go again."

"But Philippe . . ."

"You see. 'But.' Always but."

"But really, Philippe . . ."

"But!"

"But-but-but-but-but-but!"

"Simmer down, anyone would think I was out with a nut."

"You're out with a sheep. Isn't that what you want?"

"Don't be silly."

"I'm a woman, I have a right to be silly."

"Yes, but not to abuse your right," he says, but he's charmed all the same.

"And how would I know when I'm abusing it, poor creature that I am?"

"You'll know when I say so."

"Oh fine. At least that's simple."

"Yes indeed, it is simple. You see. It's very simple."

He repeats: "It's very simple." He looks at me without speaking for a moment, and then goes on:

"Doesn't that simplicity mean anything to you? Doesn't it speak to you? You've never known anything like it before. You've never wanted to know it. It's a whole part of life you know nothing about. That total surrender to love which you refuse so fiercely has great joys to offer. And you're in danger of never experiencing them. . . ."

"But that would be a Carmel!"

"A Carmel with the man you love, does that frighten you so? If you really loved me, Céline, such a Carmel would look like paradise to you! Your dearest wish! If you don't want it, it's plain enough that you don't love me. How about it?"

"Philippe . . . I love you . . ."

"All right. Do you want to love me—completely? Otherwise, I . . ."

"But why, Philippe . . . why can't we go on . . ."

"Because I'm not kidding! I don't play around with love! You *are* kidding. You're playing. You don't give, you only lend! And I'm not interested in borrowing! You can take yourself back if you're only on loan! And you can do it right now! You still haven't answered the question I just asked you. God knows it's clear enough! Anyway, I can't wait around any more. If it's yes, it has to be all the way. Or else—or else you can go back to living your way. Go back to your freedom if it's so dear to you. Take care of yourself again, with the same brilliant results you've had up to now. Isn't that true? Twenty-seven is a fine age to make a start. By that time one has a pretty good idea of one's capacities. One can draw up a little balance sheet. Success or failure. I don't know how yours would come out. . . . But Céline . . . What's the matter? Where are you going?"

Where am I going?

"I did the right thing to come here. I was afraid I'd find you in bad shape. Céline. Céline look. Look at me. My poor baby. Your poor eyes . . ."

16

He takes some damp cloths and puts them on my forehead. He sits on the edge of the bed where I lie crumpled, my head in the pillows.

"There, there. That's it. Just take it easy. I'm here. Are you glad I'm here? Come closer. That's it. Lean on me. You're safe here."

I had run away from him—and there was nothing left afterwards. My twenty-seven years and nothing else. Empty-handed. Nothingness. And not even him any more. Nothing.

"There, there, it's all over now, it's all right, you'll see, everything will be easy. Hush now. Quiet. Ah, it's a good thing I thought it over, didn't take it seriously when you ran away, didn't give up. . . . I was desperate at first, you know. . . . When I saw you leave . . . You went like a frightened little animal, you left everything behind you, your purse, your coat. And in that cold. That's what changed my mind. Look, Céline, try to rest. I hope you haven't caught something. . . . You're burning up. . . ."

He goes to get aspirin, more damp cloths; he rocks me. But he didn't wait long before:

"You were bound to crack up sooner or later. I knew very well you had heartaches. I was pretty hard on you, but I had to be, we had to lance the abscess, it hurt you too much. Cry, cry, it will do you good. I knew I'd win out, the fortress would surrender. Oh how you fought! Your poor heavy heart my poor darling. You must realize how much you were repressing. How it was poisoning you. . . . My poor little love. You see what strong feelings you have, so strong you daren't give way to

17

them. My poor baby. Now, now. Be quiet. Try to rest. I'm here. I'm going to stay here. I love you. You don't have to be afraid any more."

In the morning he called the doctor.

"I'm here. I'll never leave you."

Oh my friends forgive me. I am lost!

PEOPLE ARE ALWAYS in a bad mood
on their wedding day. He is too. He complains because
the mayor made an idiotic speech. In his opinion. What
was he expecting? This is a wedding, not the Nobel Prize
ceremony. The mayor made an average kind of speech.
Things have been going along the way you'd expect them
to. What is surprising is that he is more surprised by this
than I am. I just smile. He asks me why I'm smiling. I tell
him that it's funny. He doesn't argue. A woman who has
just had a nervous breakdown with a two-hundred-thou-
sand-franc clinic bill must be handled with care. Yesterday he asked me Are you happy? and there went the
tears again. It seems I'm not quite well yet. That's probably why he hasn't said anything about my costume. (I
can't think of another word for it.)

What got into me? Why, with thousands to choose
from, did I pick this suit? It wasn't that I had to pinch
pennies, he was terribly generous about opening charge

accounts, with the unspoken suggestion: Make an effort for once. I made one.

This morning, looking at myself in the mirror for the last time before the Departure (Farewell, little room), I realized I was dressed in deep mourning. How had I managed that? Look at that hat. I can't say I never tried it on. I tried on fifty of them. And I chose this one. What a genius. Intuitively, like a homing pigeon, I discovered the perfect outfit to wear to the funeral of an old aunt in the country. I could have done better in any bargain basement. Just this once I didn't go to a bargain basement. I was aiming higher. That will teach me.

But what can be done now? One can't go to a wedding, especially her own, in slacks and a car coat. I have nothing else to wear, and what little I have is packed.

It was desperately late. I said to myself: I won't go. Women get these aesthetic blocks, momentous decisions can be made on a purely sartorial basis. But the thought that if I gave up I'd just have the Whole Thing to do over got me going. I dried my tears and repaired my eye make-up which I'd applied generously just for this day to accentuate the funereal effect. I looked awful. The only advice I could give myself was to avoid mirrors. I was late, the car was waiting, and so was the witness I had invited in the absence of any family.

I had no family but he had plenty. Of course they were on hand to see me arrive. I saw my disaster reflected in their eyes; his shame reflected in his. He hadn't expected this. I hadn't either, but how could I explain it to him? Out of delicacy, no one brought up the subject. If only I could fade into the background! It isn't easy when you're the bride.

His Mother is completely overcome with pity. Poor girl (me). Her son is marrying a pitiful orphan who doesn't even know how to dress. One must brace oneself for such things when one has children. They're bound to pick up God knows who or what, and these days, with the break-down of classes, you can't even admit your shock without seeming reactionary. She thinks of the Nice Girls who would have asked for nothing better in life than a hand-some boy like Philippe, girls with whom he could have had a Real Marriage, with an announcement in *Figaro*, maybe even a photograph with it, instead of this surrep-titious hole-in-corner affair. But then she has second thoughts: naïf as he is, slave to his senses, he might have been caught by an out-and-out prostitute, and at least he's spared her that. She embraces me sadly. She is wearing a natural raw silk coat; her sister Irène is in pastel shantung; Stephanie is in a white embroidered dress suitable to her age; and my own Camille, my witness and only support (not my best friend but my most presentable one, whom I chose for everyone's sake—I was a big enough blot on the landscape, and just because you've got trouble your-self there's no reason to drag your pals into it), is wearing an adorable new confection in flame pink so that every-one takes her for the bride: how could anyone in his right mind believe the real one is this country cousin in deep mourning trying to hide behind the furniture? I caught Madame Aignan giving Camille a wistful look: if only he had chosen that one! . . . In short, I'm the only one in black in the midst of this veritable flower bed, only me in black wool on this radiant spring morning, and to cap the climax, it's a beautiful day. I wish desperately that it would rain. Anyway, isn't it the superstition that rain is lucky for a marriage? Not a drop fell on this one. Not all day.

What a day. We were dead before it began. Documents: the sight of a document gives me the colic. Errands: it is incredible the things one has to buy in order to get married, and the reasons one has to buy them. Passports: get out of town as soon as the thing's over, it seems it can't wait, as if the mayor's office were an assembly line. The Notary: the contract for the Separation of Property, so important for the rich in France; that's the craziest; one moment we're united, the next we're separated; what's separated? His Property from my No-Property, eternal Love but precautions just in case, Total Surrender but wait a minute, not of everything! Since I had just come out of a madhouse I felt at home immediately. With all that I had arrived at my wedding half dead. These things really kill me. I'll never do this again, that's for sure. Or else I'll hire a secretary to serve as proxy.

Yesterday I had to go to confession to get the certificate needed for church ceremonies. Marriage is only for those proven purified. I said to Philippe:

"What am I supposed to say to this character? Give me an idea."

"Look, I can't tell you what to confess!"

"What are you going to tell him?"

"None of your business!"

My God, is he going to take it seriously? Everything he ever said before made me assume he was a freethinker, and besides, he belongs to the radical party—the newest version, but just the same . . .

"Okay, I'll tell him I stole apples. Otherwise it will go on for six months and he'll refuse me absolution at the end. And the certificate too. I'll have to invent something. I'll read Joyce to him. And I don't even remember the *Confiteor*. I confess to Almighty God and to Jesus Christ His only begotten son, to blessed Mary ever virgin and to all the saints—I'll mix it up with the *Credo*, I know I will— that I have grievously sinned in thought, word, and deed —there, that's better—*mea culpa, mea culpa*. . . . Look, do I really have to?"

He's as nervous as a second assistant movie director, almost runs into a bus, and gets himself called pansy for his pains. I laugh. He doesn't like my laughing. I take this opportunity to say that I hear a rattle in the motor, which is my system with crazy drivers. It cools them off. I'm desperate but I'd hate such a stupid death. He listens to his motor all the way to the Place Saint-Sulpice. Which, it seems, is my parish church. I hesitate on the threshold. I know it's going to be cold in there. The only time I ever went in was to fix my stocking when my garter broke. It was cold then. I say:

"It's a headache to have to go in there. Why must I put up with all this nonsense?"

"You know perfectly well it's for my family's sake. We've gone over this before, I can't see why you're bringing it up again."

"Because now it's staring me in the face. Is your family really religious?"

23

"A civil marriage would embarrass them. I see no reason for embarrassing them."

"It's frightening."

"What's frightening?"

"If you have children will they have to get married in church so as not to embarrass you? That kind of thing can go on until the end of time, no one will know who God is any more but it will still go on. Don't you find that frightening?"

"What do you expect?"

"I expect to find God in church, is there something peculiar about that?"

"That's not the point. We have to have the certificate showing you've confessed, that's all. There's nothing metaphysical about it. Why don't you grow up? Go on in, we can't wait here on the steps for you to have a spiritual awakening. We have a lot to do today."

"I hate doing it. It's a rotten thing to do."

"You should have thought of that before."

"Well, now I have thought of it. My feet don't want it."

"If you do metaphysics with your feet nothing else can surprise me. In any case it's too late, the papers are made out, the appointment is made. It's even paid for."

"Oh, it's paid for, is it? Fine. Listen, I really must love you if it's making me drag myself into a church. Seriously, Philippe, I want you to recognize this as a real proof of love."

"My dear girl, do let's be a little logical. Either you don't believe these things are important—as you pretend —and so it doesn't matter to you whether or not you drag yourself into a church, as you put it, or, if it does matter to you, then you do believe it is important, in which case you should stop pretending to be so strong-minded. Be a little honest."

After that there was nothing to do but shut up.

"You know what I came for the last time I was here?"

"No, and I don't want to. Once and for all I give you my permission to keep such confidences to yourself."

What can he have imagined?

The bells are ringing. It's a lovely day. I'm married.

"You don't look very happy," says Camille, who's having a lousy time too, it's a dirty trick to have made her come but I had to have somebody.

"I shouldn't have gotten married in a church."

"Typical of you. Now that it's over."

"How was I supposed to know it before I went in?"

I shouldn't have gone against my principles just to please Madame Aignan. Madame Aignan isn't worth such a compromise. Nor is anyone else. I just shouldn't have done it. I made a mistake. But from what God can I ask forgiveness and mercy? Christians are lucky, they have someone. We have to get along by ourselves. I'm not going to forgive myself for this. His reasoning was false. I was taken in. Am I going to have to be excommunicated by Rome, now, just to straighten things out?

They say love is an excuse for anything. I'm not so sure. All right, let's go. Philippe—ah, he's here?—opens the portière for me ceremoniously. I think I have a run in my stocking. Take it easy, there's only the luncheon to get through. . . . And after that, life. To our Carmel, driver.

"Well, we've a lovely day for it," says Irène, as we arrive at the Aignans' where the luncheon is to be held because the bride has no family. "Not a cloud. That's unusual for this time of year. We're lucky."

"Isn't it supposed to rain on a happy marriage?" says Bruno, whom Big Brother's wedding hasn't sweetened up in the least. "It seems to me I've heard that."

"I can't imagine where—how can you say such a thing?" his mother replies. "There's no such saying. You must have made it up."

"I've heard it," says Bruno.

"I have too, Mama," says Stephanie.

"It's an old wives' tale," says their mother, with a murderous look which her cherubs ignore.

"Maybe in the country," says Irène, trying to smooth things over.

"No, in the movies," says Stephanie.

"I meant," says Irène, "that it may be a saying in the country because the weather is more important there. For farming. But here . . ."

"You aren't too tired, are you, Céline?" asks Madame Aignan, trying to change the subject.

I'm exhausted. Beat. But what have I done? Nothing really. Gotten married. Where is Philippe? Talking to his father. Get married and you don't know each other any more. When I think that we used to sleep together! When I saw him coming in those days, my heart would leap for joy. What am I doing here? I don't even know anybody except Camille, to whom I stick like a barnacle.

"You look lost, my poor child."

"I am. I don't know a soul here. Could we go somewhere else?"

"On you marriage doesn't look so good. What made you do it?"

"I can't remember any more. Something to do with oysters. Then I went to sleep. I think I had shock treatment too. I woke up today, in deep mourning; too late, the mass was paid for."

I can't say I'm really awake even now. Come make yourself comfortable, says Madame Aignan, who can't stand seeing me there like a piece of furniture. I take off my jacket and am revealed in a romantic blouse with ruffles; I look like Harpo Marx in drag. What in God's name was I thinking of when I bought this? Did I think that the habit would make the monk? This whole thing is a tragedy of good intentions: I really wanted to dress like a bride but I simply haven't got what it takes. I put my jacket back on; maybe it's less terrible that way; the only other possibility is to undress completely. I caught Madame Aignan gazing at my stomach. Naturally. She was expecting it to show about five months; why else would anyone have married a thing like me? No, dear Madame, I'm flat as a pancake; I have both contraceptives and principles. Then it must be pity, she answers (I am telepathic in simple cases like this), for a poor sick girl just out of a sleep cure at the clinic, supposedly suffering from a nervous breakdown which was probably a suicide attempt planned in order to hook my son just as he was ready to leave her for one of those innumerable nice girls who would have asked nothing better—and who parenthetically, dear Madame, screw around happily with the professional beatniks at parties in the Latin Quarter, I've even run across some of them going to it in telephone booths, and far be it from me to reproach them—one way or another my poor son was taken in by blackmail thinks his mother. I smile at her. Dear Madame, your son is marrying me for love, it's sad but true.

I feel somewhat better without my hat. I comb my hair with my fingers as usual. I almost begin to feel like myself. I put lots of water in my whisky. I'm thirsty. Who can I ask where the powder room is? I ask Stephanie; at her age one still understands life. She leads me down an endless corridor.

"Is it far? I can hardly walk. I've thought of nothing else since we were at the mayor's office."

"Even when you were saying Yes?"

"That's when it began."

She gives me a startled look: is my appearance deceptive? Her eyes are questioning; lovely insolent eyes, I try to respond to them. Finally we are there. When I come out again she is still waiting: sometimes you get lost in this place; feeling better? Yes, now I'll be able to drink. To forget? she says. I don't know, I don't even know what I'm supposed to forget any more. She laughs. What did you do before? Little girls are funny. Before what? Before you married Philippe. Strip teaser. Oh, says Stephanie admiringly, now I know what's bugging Mama. She doesn't know it, I say. We concealed it. I see, says Stephanie, that's really better, I won't tell either you can count on me. Oh, it's not important now I say, I don't think I'll go on with it, Philippe doesn't want me to, he says he earns enough to support us both. Do you earn a lot as a strip teaser? Oh, you make out. It's funny, you marrying Philippe, she says. Yes, isn't it?—I think so too.

As we enter the salon we hear a dire melody: Tam, tam, tatam, tam tatam, tatam, tatam . . .

"Bruno!" cries his mother. "What's that?"

"What's what?" he says. "It's the wedding march. Oh shit, I put it on the wrong side, it's the funeral one. Sorry," he says to me. He notices that I think it's funny and stares openmouthed.

"Never mind," I say. "It's nice too. I like music." "Is there something you'd like to hear?" he asks. "The Eroica maybe?" I say. "Or some Brassens . . . Oh, have you any Bop?"

"Now?" asks Bruno.

"Maybe later?"

I'm sitting on the floor with Stephanie; we go through the records; we're already less bored. Stephanie wants a song of Ferré's, "you know the one about the guy who lays the maid and eats dandelion greens? They'll be mad. We'll have some kicks."

"Luncheon is served, madame."

"I suppose Madame is me?"

"Shit," says Bruno, "just when we were beginning to have fun."

I've often noticed that the bourgeois serve awful food. And they don't pass the dishes often enough. You wonder what they plan to do with the leftovers. Even at a wed-

ding. They had it all done by a caterer, fancy, but over-
cooked. Well, that's life, as Philippe says. The two kids
down at the other end of the table catch my eye from
time to time, which is a lifesaver, because the others . . .

Philippe and his family have just about exhausted the
theme of the Honeymoon Trip, Philippe knows just
what places we'll be passing through and what we'll see
there, it's hardly worth going any more. I haven't joined
in, I'm not up on geography, that's my weak spot, my
strong one is math, which is not much help conversation-
ally. The older generation, by a process of Association of
Ideas, have dug up corresponding memories, the Windmill
country the Tulips and the Fjords; Nowadays one is
more likely to go south, it's warmer, says Irène, and
Philippe adds that there's the sea, in the North too says
Madame Aignan, yes but it's not the same, in the south it's
the Mediterranean says Irène, nowadays it's chic to go to
the Mediterranean even at this time of year so long as
there isn't that horrible July crowd, and the prices are
lower too, the prices, you have to take advantage of that,
there are the mountains too says Monsieur Aignan, I like
the mountains they're healthy, and the air is so good, and
it's fashionable there too especially in spring when the
winter crowds have left, but for a Honeymoon Trip suggests Madame Aignan, the mountains might not be quite
the thing. Why? asks Irène. Why not? You wear yourself
out says Bruno which doesn't exactly serve your purpose,
I'd rather have gone to Spain cuts in Philippe irritated by
his brother's interruption, but Céline doesn't like Spain, at
this there is general consternation, what you don't like
Spain, how can anyone not like Spain! Do you know it?

they ask me, you really have to get to know it well, there are little places where the tourists never go that's where you have to explore, have you been there? No. That's the first time I've opened my mouth. But if you've never been there? Philippe smiles indulgently and takes my hand: She doesn't like it. I don't like Flamenco, I say, What, you don't like Flamenco it's so beautiful! cries Irène, and the others chime in how they love Flamenco all French people have it in their blood, you can tell by the way they clap their hands like real gypsies when they're in the Guitare or the Barrio Chino de Paris, and then Spain is so cheap says Madame Aignan. Anyway, I don't like bullfights I say, But you've never seen one says Irène, wait till you've seen one, how do you know? I didn't think I'd like it because it's so cruel and then I saw one and I was caught. By whom? says Bruno, Bruno! says his father in a tone of soft reproach suitable to the solemnity of this day which he doesn't want to spoil, Irène laughs to show she isn't angry, and begins a description of the time she Lost Control at the bullfight (haha) and threw her gloves in the ring, and there was one which hooked onto the horn of the bull (the poor animal looked so silly). Maybe if they'd guarantee that the torero would be put to death I'd go, I say firmly, she's sadistic this child! Irène exclaims tenderly. They're really marvelous. But you don't know the rules, says Monsieur Aignan, who proceeds to explain them to me because he knows them backwards and forwards the only thing missing is that he's never been in the ring and put them into practice. And then Spain really isn't expensive says Madame Aignan forgetting she's already said this, Yugoslavia isn't either says Philippe, and they're off again on exchange, and the Cost of Living in every corner of the earth, based, of course it's obvious on the ratio of the workingman's wage to the price of a kilo of bread, and they can analyze the centavo for you in such a way that in a week of knowledgeable manipulations they realize a ten per cent profit, at that point I lose them for a moment while I eat my croquette and I pick them up again at the Prosperity of France, the Tancarville Bridge, Southern Thruway and our great Atomic Center. When I finally get tired of listening to this crap I announce: all this is going to crash you know because the system is basically rotten, you know what they call the situation in France in the foreign press, don't you? Inflation. Don't you read the foreign papers? Silence, and the father, who is now mine too, looks at me thoughtfully a moment, telling himself that on my wedding day it's too early to tell me to button my lip, so, throwing me a paternal smile, he says: We're boring this child with all these difficult subjects, she's right to call our attention to it, I hope it will be warm enough for you to swim down there? She's taking her snorkel, Philippe puts in quickly with tenderness. Really? says his father admiringly, so you have a spear fisherman in the family? Oh no! I say. I only look. I never want to kill any fish. I hate hunting of every kind as a pastime it's silly and uselessly expensive, and completely phony. Phony! he cries, not happy at all at this and forgetting the sanctity of the day because he goes hunting every fall which I knew very well but wanted to liven things up before I died of boredom. I continue to egg him on: Those poor pheasants who are practically hand fed all year to the point where they come running like chickens when they're called and then one fine day a bunch of armed men comes and fires on them without warning, do you call that sport? Céline, murmurs Philippe through his teeth but now that I've managed to come to life a bit I'm not about to relapse, I'm not in the habit of putting up with this kind of thing, ordinarily in such cases I take a powder but this time I can't so I have to do something. Have you ever gone? asks Irène, sneakily this time, she's beginning to catch on that I've never gone anywhere (anywhere that's anywhere). I'll say I haven't! I say disdainfully. Then you can't know, says Irène. She speaks from her heart, says Monsieur Aignan who has a grip on himself once more, but I: I can understand why they hunt stag with a spear. Then I don't understand you at all, says the father, if you are so sensitive, how you can stand the spear. . . . I tell you, she's sadistic, says Irène maliciously. Philippe is dying of embarrassment; I'm making gaffe after gaffe, he doesn't know how to stop me, I'm going to be black and blue where he's kicking me. You can't expect my father to hunt stag says Bruno, he would never come back; even pheasant hunting can be dangerous, a man was killed at it not long ago. It was a hunter who killed him, not a pheasant, says Stephanie. Never mind, says Bruno, I'd feel safer about him if he'd limit his shooting to craps. Look, says his mother. You don't know how dangerous a stag can be when he charges, our September Nimrod tells me, ignoring the children. Well, that's just what makes it interesting, it wouldn't be sport otherwise. I told you, says Irène coming in again. First she wants to kill the bullfighter, now the hunter! She's a sadist. Here's the dessert, says Madame Aignan as if we could miss this ten-layer monstrosity, but her strategy succeeds and everyone looks at the cake, You must cut it, Céline. That's enough champagne Philippe whispers as the bottle is passed, you're tight enough. Your health, says his father, bound that the day will be full of merrymaking no matter what, he lifts his glass, to your good health, both of you, Madame Aignan dries a purely conventional tear, may it last longer than mine, says Cousin Aimée shedding a good many, her husband just died of cancer as she so graphically informed us over the hors d'oeuvres in full detail, a carcinoma of the intestine, we raise our glasses, and just then, from the next room we hear a melody which I know well, with its familiar words, "There is no happy love." Innocently Bruno returns to his place at the table. That boy is right on the ball and someday I'm going to tell him so.

The test of a good song is whether everybody, even the fools, shut up while it's sung. We listen, in religious silence.

Unexpectedly tears come to my eyes. It happens to me rather a lot lately. I wonder where they come from.

It's time to go! Philippe is calling in my ear. Was I asleep? Anyway, he isn't calling, he's murmuring, really; I am on a couch. A hospital, maybe. No, it's a room, Empire style with lots of crystal dangles. Horribly ugly; greenish; nauseating. . . . Not very stable emotionally, just come out of a nervous breakdown; tell me, do you think it might have been a suicide attempt? say voices, among whom I recognize one, Sssh says Philippe she's awake, that was Madame Aignan before now she comes forward, feeling better? Yes yes says Philippe impatiently, we'll be along to say good-by right away, we'll follow you, run along, I've told you not to drink so much, he says to me the moment we're alone, you know you can't take it any more! And today of all days! I'd hoped you could at least control yourself. At least for today! But that was too much to ask. He paces the room furiously.

Okay, now I know what's going on. The old story. The question is what did I do. I can imagine. People have already told me that I have lots of ideas at such moments. Better not ask questions just now. From the look of him I've done a fine job of it.

"Are you capable of standing? Without staggering? Shall we see?" I walk the lines of the floor boards. I think I do very well, I follow them exactly.

I acquit myself just as honorably crossing the living room and it's a big one, too; Philippe doesn't need to clutch my arm that way, he's confusing being a few sheets to the wind with having polio; he's hurting me. The great room looks like a desert compared to what it was at the cocktail hour, when it was full. Oh Lord, have I gone through a whole cocktail party without knowing it? It's a bore to be quite that vague. Stephanie's face gladdens when she sees me: if only I could read what is written there! she, at any rate, seems to have happy memories of this cocktail party. What a shame you have to leave says Bruno with an understanding look, but understanding what? I'll be back, I say in order to say something. I hope so he answers, as far as I'm concerned you're always welcome. Ouch, it must have been bad. Monsieur Aignan, Father, kisses me however, but very coldly; I hope this lovely trip will put you back on your feet he says, be sure and get a good rest. There's a Band-Aid on his cheek that wasn't there before, where did that come from? You'll have to excuse her, Papa, says Philippe, she's still very, she's still a little . . . Of course I excuse her says his father (for what, oh Lord?), on a day like this everything is excused, I understand completely my boy it's forgotten, come now, have a good time children and come back to us in good form!

The last hedge before the finish line is Madame Aignan; she shakes off the cancer victim's widow, who seems to be glued to her, in order to embrace her son; she sniffles; Come on now Mama says Philippe, come on, I'm not going off to war. She's not so sure of that. Her cheek is wet; it isn't a hedge, it's the water jump; fortunately she doesn't kiss me at length, there seems to be a lack of enthusiasm. Now it's over. No, I can't escape the widow of the carcinoma, she has been waiting for this moment to let her heart run over, she didn't want to darken such a day, but just the same she can't help saying how hard it is for one who has just suffered such a loss to see Youth and Happiness Embarking on Life, she hopes ours will be a long, long, long, long one, Madame Aignan pries her loose before she reaches eternity and pulls Philippe aside to give him heaven knows what last bit of good advice. I can stand up pretty well without him. Someone lends me a handkerchief to dry the tears of the Widow from the face of the Bride—it wasn't Veronica, it was Camille, who seems in great shape, How come you're still here you looked as if you'd just about had it the last time I saw you, I found a reason for staying she says and looks at Bruno, who looks back with a free and easy smile. Ah. Camille is a fast worker. So was I in bygone days. Bygone days. Congratulations. To you too she says, you were marvelous. Me? How? What did I do? Go to bed with someone? Who? No, besides with whom, except your husband, since I was hanging onto Bruno, no, but you were marvelous just the same. Especially the sermon about Carmel. Lord! And the hunt for huntsmen was great too, did we ever laugh, the three of us anyway. Not the others. As for the strip tease . . .

"Are you coming?" says Philippe.

"Good-by," says Camille, "and congratulations for the mourning weeds too, you were damned courageous to do it."

"Wasn't I? that's what I said to myself too, when I realized it this morning. . . ."

"Are you coming?" says Philippe.

Never has the thought of making love been farther from my mind. Never!

I want to sleep. To rest. What a day. I'm dead. Exhausted. Getting married is a shock, don't you agree? You can't just swallow it like a pill. I've changed my whole life. It's tiring. I'm worn out. I want to sleep. And then the champagne, on top of the other wine; those wines, their passion for mixtures, you could die of it.

Always before when Philippe and I went to bed it was to make love. Otherwise we slept in our own rooms. Now and henceforth there will only be one bed to sleep in. He's already in it. I join him. I'd like to sleep. Or maybe not sleep. Think. Dream. Settle down. I don't know. I'd like some time. To put myself together again. Collect my wits. Or talk, maybe? I don't know. Here he is on top of me.

All right. If he doesn't understand that much I can't explain it to him. It's too long and complicated. Let it go, it doesn't really matter, a man who's been my lover for the last six months. Let's be simple. Let it pass.

Easy to say. But. One still has to. And he: "What's the matter?"

Me:

"Nothing. . . . Maybe I'm a little tired. . . ."

And he:

"Already?"

So there we are. Cut. Finished. Dead. The abyss. When you get there, there's no place left to go. It's too late. He should have understood. In life there's only one way to understand each other: just understand. Without that, nothing is any good, not explanations or anything. All you can do then is try to forget. That's what I tried. But not everything can be controlled, you can't reason with the body, things are the way they are: for your body: mine wasn't very receptive. Nothing to be done about it. I finally ask myself what prostitutes do. They must have a trick. Otherwise it's just not possible. Anyway for me. If I'm not in the mood it's murder.

He's withdrawn to the other side of the bed; his back is turned. Clothed in the dignity of an offended husband. Of a husband; that's the only thing that's important to him.

38

Can't you understand? Can't you understand? Can't you understand? Can't you see? At least see a little? It's so obvious. Do you expect me to be fresh as a daisy after a day like this? Do you by any chance think the effect of your family is aphrodisiac? If you had any sense you'd at least give me a week to digest them. And the trip in the car on top of it, two hundred kilometers at night at 140 in utter silence, Monsieur righteously at the wheel not saying a word, thus demonstrating his disgust for the drunk in the bucket seat, where she was thrown with a brutality which would have elicited a couple of slaps from anyone less cowardly than me—if you think this is calculated to give a girl hot pants think again. What do they imagine we are? What do they think we're made of? Meat? And afterwards in bed not a gesture, not a word to help you forget it, not, It was a hard day, wasn't it? or At last it's over, or something a little human at least? In the past you never would have come to me without some gentleness, never, in the past. . . .

Ah but the past is the past. Today you're my husband. Fool. No more favors: rights. And they're waiting to see which way the cat is going to jump, oh yes. They're waiting to see what she's going to do now that they're married. Now that he's married me. Haha. They're waiting to see, their minds all made up. —"Already?"—that was an instant response, it was all prepared. And it was a low blow. Oh vile man! Now on the other side of the bed, very far away. Let him stay there.

Oh but my heart. One more thing I can't control, oh damn this body, my heart bangs against all my bones, my solar plexus is in a knot, my gorge is rising, the clinical picture is complete, my chest is hollow, the death rattle will come next. I'm in agony. I can't bear it. It's not possible. This has to stop or I'll die. Can someone bring me some smelling salts? No, this is serious, I'm really dying. I love him! Philippe!

Now what shall I do? I'll leave, there's nothing else left. It's all impossible. All right, up. Get up. You hear me, body? But it doesn't want to. The poor thing is suffering. It hurts. Gnagnagna. There it is, it's crying. In a minute it will be calling for its papa and mama. There it goes, it's speaking, it says: "Philippe, please . . ."

"I'm tired."

Anyway he's not asleep. Well, he answers. Stupidly, but he answers, all is not lost.

"Well you should be. I'd have understood your being tired."

"You've had time to think up some good excuses?"

What a bore. Half of me would rather be a hundred miles away than here dealing with this nonsense. But the other half doesn't want to move an inch. Not for the world. My second half would kill my first half if it tried to leave; that's just what it does now. It repeats, "Philippe, please," it seems that's all it knows how to say. But it works. He moves. If I wanted to be clever this would be the moment to turn *my* back, if I were more of a whore. But I'm not clever, I'm not a whore, I love. Oh shit. My body moves too.

"All of a sudden you aren't tired any more?"
"No."

Let's skip a little. The truth is that I'm exhausted and not really in the mood, but to hell with that, this isn't the place for it. The rest is up to Nature, which isn't too particular. What a job. Please God let my damned body be a little more biddable. I think he must have decided it would be better not to linger over details this time. He's afraid too. Which of us is more afraid? Oh, love is lovely. Afterwards, all I have to do is have confidence; luckily he has the magic touch; after all, that's what made me fall for him. There aren't many like that: it's a rare surprise. Some people will know what I mean. The day after that "surprise," with him better known as Love, I went off to find Thomas and I said to him: "I can't help it, he has the magic touch." I had to explain. You can't fall madly in love with another man when you're in the middle of a charming affair without offering some explanation. I was still innocent then, it never occurred to me that this meant the affair would have to be broken off forever; I did think that Thomas, who was a good friend, the kind one keeps, might be a little touchy during the first raptures of my new passion, but then, one day, sooner or later, every-thing would fall back into what I call order, and Philippe calls disorder; and life would go on. "And were you happy like that?" Well, I wasn't unhappy. The question never came up. I lived. Things went along naturally; I took them in my stride; we passed on, or else they passed on. At that time everything came naturally. We loved all the time, and was it really necessary to know whom? I loved cities because of certain people. "And can you tell me what's left after all that?" Well, cities are left; music wine smells colors sounds lights; life itself is left. Myself. And something more, something you didn't have before, something you only have if you've slept around a lot

41

when you're just young enough. Something that has to do with love, but which is bigger. That's all I know, I never had time to complete my studies. The sacrifice of Thomas was exacted of me, it must be total, I was never to meet him again. I didn't mind the others, they were just passing things anyway. "You must choose between him and me." Instant ultimatum. Violence. Hurry. What a way to live. That's Occidentals for you. They can't let things happen the way they want to. We could have waited to see, no? No. Things have to happen the way they want them to. Sometimes it works. Seems to. It's by this means among others that they've conquered the world. Yes but, at what price? all you have to do is look at it. Thomas was sacrificed, what else could I do? I was trapped. That's the way they make us lose our innocence. What's so sad he says, is not just losing you, but losing you in such a stupid way. I understand how you feel—but what is love? Where does passion come from?—and where does it go? I didn't know either. Thomas was sacrificed but at what price only time will tell. Men look before they leap and then discover the consequences when they are crushed by them. Where does passion come from? Where does it go? Why is my body here with my hurt spirit inside it? I was thinking while in Philippe's arms, even the magic touch leaves a little of you to go on thinking and anyway making love inspires me, it clarifies my ideas. We left at dawn on schedule, having barely closed our eyes. He'd had it, his Wedding Night.

THE WOMAN WHO has never in her life chosen curtains cannot know. They are overpowering. You may think yourself strong, but curtains are stronger. You begin by sneering at the whole thing, you behave as if it were someone else you were watching with amusement, choosing curtains, some other woman whom we'll suppose is your servant, because you could never get that excited about choosing curtains, you're above that. And then wham. There you are. What happened? You didn't have time to catch it, any more than one catches oneself falling asleep. You've become the type who chooses curtains, you are the servant, the two of you are one, you've entirely forgotten the existence of the other who was yourself. You are swallowed up. Very important, the choice of curtains. The color; the fabric; the hang of the fabric (you start using words like hang!); should they be lined or not? Very important. Everything is very important. The heavy fabrics are all so ugly they make you

43

want to vomit; what won't they think of next? They're in business for the perversion of taste. The home furnishings floor is a museum of horrors. "But madame, we sell a lot of it," that's the key argument. What the hell do I care what other people like? Don't you have anything simple for those of us who are still sane? You understand, simple? "But madame, this is what they're making." That's what the manufacturers are making, I can see that, but how about what the customer wants, does anyone care about that or not? We sell a great deal of it, madame. My God, what do you expect people to buy here except what you have? It's unbelievable. Unbearable. It's tyranny. Curtains, madame? Better look in home furnishings. I just left there. They haven't a thing. Nothing? The dumfounded saleswoman surveys the enormous area of the condemned floor. But madame, that fabric isn't for curtains, that's for lining. And what made you decide that it was lining? If I hang it at my windows won't it be curtains? Pure semantics. People are taken in. They don't know what a thing is any more, they only know its name. I bought sateen to prove my point, and the saleswoman was upset. And now the bedspread, should it or should it not match the curtains? Read *France-Femme* and learn how to live. I'd like that in the 54-inch width. It doesn't come in that width, madame. What do you mean, it doesn't come in that width? You need it in that width. We only carry the 36-inch width in this department. That's idiotic! That's how it is. How many widths will I need for a bedspread, then? Oh, you want the bedding department, madame, if it's for a bedspread. Bedding for beds. They find it shocking that I should look for it among

44

the curtain materials, that I should have escaped from their prison of words. That I ask for what I want and don't just accept what they offer me. How can I be so stupid that I don't know it's demand which responds to supply, not supply to demand? Either they know the system is upside down, or they don't know because they're upside down with it. It isn't their fault; the system pays their wages. Underpaid, always on their feet, even needing permission to take a leak, human beings are marked-down merchandise here. Tonight she'll say to her husband, I waited on a real nut today. I suppose she's right, I've been seeking the light of logic in the Marts of Trade. I'd like some cotton voile without hemstitching. They don't make it, madame. Why? Because this is the way it's made, madame. And why is it made this way? She's getting angry. There's no demand for it, madame. But didn't I just ask you for it? No, that's not it: since there's no demand for it, I, who just asked for it, must not exist. They're just waiting for me to go away. It's a subtle way of turning men into sheep. I'll have no curtains if it goes on like this. Or else I'll have to give in. They're getting to me. They're strong. They've decided that this year my saucepans will be tangerine, turquoise, or tortoise shell, just like other women's. No exceptions for me. Because if people were left alone the fools would buy their saucepans once for all and then what would happen to business? Steps must be taken against all those lazy idiots who would still be living in trees and picking fruit if they weren't shaken up once in a while. You have to present them with new things constantly to make them spend a buck, they're so tight. I don't know if you've noticed

45

it but purses and bathing suits are also tangerine this year, and if you'll check in *France-Femme* you'll see on every page that it's the last word and if you aren't wearing it you'll look like a square. It's a command. These In colors are coming at me from every point of the compass, violating my eyes, burying themselves in my brain. Actually they aren't so bad; they come in tones you can only call studied, Committees of Co-ordination have spent hours over them, and you can bet that's not for nothing, those gentlemen aren't types who are about to waste time over the rainbow . . . and, as if by magic, you can't find any more pale blue saucepans like the ones I wanted, not in any department; They don't make them any more, madame—shall I wear myself out in useless research, become an archaeologist of saucepans out of pure stubbornness? Holding out that way would be even stupider, and then what the hell do I really care what color my saucepans are? I'll never see them, I'll have a maid. I go home with a set of the tortoise shell, exhausted, on the verge of tears, beaten by the system.

"I don't understand how you can act out a Greek tragedy in a department store," says Philippe. "You're the only one who could manage it. It must be exhaustion."

"But hemstitching is lovely," says Madame Aignan. "Especially for a bedroom. But if you like the plain better, you could have nylon voile, which is much easier to wash, and you hardly have to iron it."

Madame Aignan (née Rabu—a good family, they say) talks like my saleswoman: they have the same syntax.

Which is perfectly natural, they're both in business, big or little doesn't make much difference.

"They don't make nylon in white. I want white."

"You do have odd ideas."

"After all, madame, when you really care . . ."

Philippe throws me a steely look: I called her madame again, I'll never get used to it. Mother sticks in my throat: she's not my mother; I don't like misusing words that way. But she looks at me affectionately anyway: our little girl is getting housebroken at last, she's worrying about something, she cares about her little home. My home. At the moment, while we wait for the painters the masons the carpenters the plumbers, that army of parasites, as Madame Aignan says, to finish up there at the Rue de la Pompe, and it won't be tomorrow either says Madame Aignan the French worker is not only the most expensive but the slowest in the world, and not the best either adds Irène, you should get Spanish or Greeks you can get them for a song, but the receipts says Philippe, without a receipt for taxes I'll be in trouble, anyway, in the meantime we're staying at the Aignans', in Philippe's old room, Empire with crystal dangles, bringing back unhappy memories which seem courteously forgotten except by Bruno and Stephanie, who once tacked a note up on the door of the newlyweds reading: Carmel, which I promptly transferred to the door of the communal john, whence some pious hand shortly removed it; who saw it and who didn't while it was up remains a mystery, these are well brought-up people. We badly brought-up ones have acquired the habit of saying, "I'm going to Carmel," when we go there. I'm lucky to have Bruno and Stephanie in my corner, because if they weren't there . . .

"Of course I understand you, you're young and it's important to you, I was the same way when I was married. I had my little quirks, didn't I, Charles?"

"Hmmm."

"But this isn't just a whim! I don't want elaborate things, I want simple ones, and I can't understand why simple things aren't made! It infuriates me."

"My dear," says Philippe, pontifical, "you must understand that Production follows certain norms . . ."

"Then we should follow them too, to be helpful."

"There goes the red flag!" he says, with an indulgent smile designed to cool me off.

"All right, so I'm a revolutionary, I don't want hemstitching."

"Have you ever thought," interrupts his father, "of what would become of us if we took each person's wishes into consideration?"

"Yes."

"Well then."

"I can't get very excited about it considering the way things are already. In chaos."

"She's an anarchist," says Irène, always ready with the *mot juste*.

"Why don't you find a good little upholsterer?" says Madame Aignan. "He could advise you. Those people are used to it. That way you'd avoid all this trouble."

"You're talking nonsense, my dear," says Philippe. "These are questions which can't be discussed without some understanding of the causative factors. It's more complicated than you think. . . ."

"Which is better: not to see the wood for the trees, or not to see the trees for the wood?"

"What?" says the whole Aignan family.

"I can understand that machines aren't flexible, that isn't exactly witchcraft," I say. "And that manufacturers are in business to make money, not to give services—God made them that way, nothing can be done about it. At the moment. I know what kind of world I live in. I can even buy nylon. What makes me sick at my stomach is that these people can't even understand a simple sentence."

"But my poor child, hasn't it dawned on you that people are stupid?" says Madame Aignan. "Take my maid Francesca, for example. She understands nothing. I can spend hours trying to explain to her."

"Maybe it's that she only understands Spanish?"

"Céline is young," says Irène. "She still has her illusions."

"I'm not sure they're so stupid. Though I'm bound to admit they're getting more so every minute. They can't help it, they're forced to do such stupid things all the time."

"You're a romantic," says Monsieur Aignan. "Rousseau."

"I don't mind being called one, but it doesn't mean I'm wrong."

"They could understand if they wanted to," says Madame Aignan. "Look at Odette's husband, he was an ordinary workman and now he's a foreman or I don't know what; he's moved up through the ranks; someday he'll be supervisor. At Simca."

"Is that where they tear up your union card when you walk in?"

"What use would you have for it?" asks Monsieur Aignan. "They have more benefits there than anywhere else. Robert is very happy. He has his own car."

"Would a workingman have had a car in the old days? The husband of our cleaning woman. You see. He can't even park in front of the factory any more because there's no space. They all have them."

"In the old days there were no cars."

"It's getting so bad nobody can drive any more," says Monsieur Aignan. "You know how long it took me to get here from the Champs Elysées? You wouldn't believe it. Even the Avenue Henri-Martin is jammed up if you try to park there."

"By workmen from Simca?"

"By them or other people. Any car takes up about the same amount of space."

"It's really scandalous," says Irène. "Something should be done about it. Rationing. Fix it so people can't buy cars so easily."

"Then what would you suggest doing with all the cars that come out of the factories?"

"What?" says Irène. "They could make fewer. More expensive ones."

"There are people who don't even have enough to eat," says Madame Aignan. "They have to feed their children on potatoes. But they have a car. They're crazy on the subject."

"And what would you do about the assembly line, Irène?"

"The what?"

"The assembly line goes on without stopping, doesn't it? And the cars come out at the other end. So you have to sell them. So credit is given to people who don't get paid enough to buy them any other way. What else can they do with them otherwise?"

"The automobile industry is one of the foremost in France!" shouts Monsieur Aignan. "It employs hundreds of thousands of people who would be on relief without it!"

"There you are, the circle is complete. You take an hour and a half to come from the Champs Elysées while I can make it in the métro in twenty minutes, and everything is for the best in this best of all capitalist worlds—"

"And of course you have the answer!" Philippe cuts in furiously. "You have found the way to regulate Production and Distribution and all, I suppose!"

"Certainly I have an answer. But it isn't mine. It's as well known as the tables of multiplication. It would have worked better a few decades ago, but it wasn't allowed. And really, it's so silly when you see what happened. Everybody would have gained by it. I mean looking at it from a point of view of pure logic."

The terrified eyes of the Aignan family converge on me. Am I—is she—what else could she be . . .

"What are you saying? What are you talking about? You're talking nonsense!" Philippe bursts out. "If you'll permit me to say so, minds a little greater than yours have been studying these problems for centuries before you came along and offered to solve everything! Who do you think you are? . . . I don't know what I'm getting so excited about," he adds, suddenly calm, with an apologetic look towards his Family, he is ashamed, "Céline is like that. She's always talking nonsense. It isn't worth getting excited about. You must be tired."

"And it all began with hemstitching," says Irène. "It's too silly."

"A whole day's shopping is really exhausting," says Madame Aignan. "Afterwards you feel like making mountains out of molehills."

"Lie down for a while," says Philippe. "Things will go back into their proper proportion."

Proportion. I take an aspirin. I'm taking a lot of them lately. It helps. My doctor—I have a doctor the way I have a Notary, now, the one who separated Philippe's Property from my No-Property, a remarkable operation that; just as I have a little dressmaker who has already turned out two miserable dresses for me, though Philippe likes them, I look like a string bean in one and a strawberry with whipped cream in the other, but the main thing is I'm no longer a disgrace at Prunier; just as I have a maid since we moved into the apartment, Spanish, and furnished by Madame Aignan, who has an inexhaustible supply of them, imported directly at very low wages, which I would like to raise a little, but Philippe was opposed to it, not that he doesn't mean well, on the contrary he's really quite a liberal, but it would have rocked the boat, and anyway it was just demagoguery on my part he said and he wasn't wrong, one shouldn't give maids raises one should cut their wages so that they'll really get fed up and man the barricades some fine day and that would be the end of it—anyway my doctor tells

me that I'm suffering from a mild chronic Agapaxia, a
disease which is characterized by sadness at unhappy
events and joy at happy ones, even, says the Dictionary of
Terminology, if said events don't concern you personally,
and which (disease which), as a result of these constant
responses, is very disruptive to the Family Circle and
which as a consequence it is necessary to cure. I'm not
kidding I read it in a book, and I asked the doctor whether
the whole world isn't off its rocker when such things are
down in black and white. He answered: You see just how
agapactic you are. Hence the difficulty on the home furnishings floor. To counteract this tendency, Madame Aignan recommended an inexpensive little upholsterer and
decorator whose address she has. The doctor, for his part,
hopes to cure me by a progressive neutralization of sensi-
tivity to be brought about by little pills, my good intentions and the Lord. In any case I threw the little pills
down the john, it's better to be careful, and I put a mild
laxative in the bottle instead, Philippe is happy so long as
I'm swallowing something and it's good for my complex-
ion. You see what leading a healthy life, going to bed
early, getting up early, not drinking too much does for
you. He says. I'm getting fat. My slacks are too tight.
Why don't you buy yourself a new dress Philippe repeats
patiently every time I ask if I can charge a new pair, you
know I never refuse you anything, but where would you
wear them? not to go out with me in, I warn you. So?
Not that he's a tightwad, he spends, but he likes to know
where it's going, and he likes to have it go where he
wants it to. My goodness I'll have to start cheating on the

accounts, I'll have to do it, it's what Julia Bigeon advises. Like maids do.

"But we all do," she says. "How would we ever get on otherwise? They're too careful about what they give us."

"It's funny, they aren't tight about other things, just about the money they give us."

"Oh well, you have to take into consideration that it's their money."

"True. They're the ones who knock themselves out making it."

"They're the ones who have the responsibilities."

"The burdens."

"The worries about the future."

"Income taxes."

"It's all on their shoulders."

"Good God, I wouldn't want to be a husband! It's one dirty job after another! Why do they do it?"

"Because they hate their solitude worse: think of them coming home to their little studios, to nothing, to nobody, alone with themselves: emptiness!"

"Poor things! they do have the worst of it. It's not much fun to be a man in this world."

"Yes. We women get to loaf around talking girl talk and shopping for dresses."

"—while they get pale in offices, out of the sun—"

"—surrounded by telephones and puffed up with importance—"

"That's their reward, after all."

"Luckily we have a war now and then so they can get a little fresh air."

"But anyway, you'll see, crooked accounts are more

fun than honest ones," says Julia. "You can make things up. You even have a good time at it. It was my mother who told me about it. She did it all her life and no one's the worse for it."

Julia is the wife of Jean-Pierre. Jean-Pierre is a friend of Philippe. He works with him at the Project, which gives them something in common, although Philippe is in Decentralization and Jean-Pierre is in Unification.

"In other words you do opposite things?"

Since we all go out together quite often, I try to be interested, to participate. No, really, I do make an effort. I want to be part of his life. I'm his wife, am I not?

"No, you don't understand, and anyway it's too long to explain to you, it's a little complicated, you see it doesn't have to do with the same things. Although in some respects they complement each other."

"Oh yes I see, that reminds me of the two architects who both had assignments to redesign a city; the one who worked on a hilltop tore down houses to make a lookout point, while the one in the valley was building skyscrapers. When they both had finished . . ."

"There's no similarity. On the contrary. My job is to institute the Decentralization of certain industries which don't really need to be in Paris and to locate them in underdeveloped regions where they will give new life and prosperity."

"Why?"

"Because otherwise these regions would be stagnant, and it isn't practical to allow waste space in a country."

"Waste space? But there are plenty of things there . . . trees. Grass."

"What are you going to do with trees and grass? They won't keep people alive. Try to follow me: look, Paris is like the sun, and the other cities are like planets which move around it. There has to be a certain harmony, understand? And that's what we're trying to bring about."

Yes, yes. Paris is a steak and the other cities are like French fries around it. Paris is like an elephant and the other cities are fleas on it, so it has to scratch itself. I do enjoy proof by analogy. I can easily think of twenty for him in case he runs short. As for the fate of a country depending on them it's poetic justice that's all I can say. And that such poetry should be under the supervision of Philippe Aignan and Jean-Pierre Bigeon is really reassuring.

"While Jean-Pierre, you see," continues my sweet dreamer, "is trying to get complementary industries to regroup themselves in a given sector . . . let's suppose . . . look . . . to give you an example . . ."

"Ducks and peas. An arms manufacturer and some men condemned to death. A cotton mill and some strip teasers. An ogre and a kindergarten."

"Horses and sparrows," says Julia.

"They aren't being serious," says Philippe. "You can never talk seriously to them."

"But that's their charm," says Jean-Pierre. "If they were different we wouldn't love them so much."

"The bigger fools we are the more they love us," says Julia.

"Don't knock it, it's restful," I say.

"You were the one who wanted it explained!" says Philippe. "And then you won't listen."

"But I understand perfectly! You're the ones who are ruining landscapes and polluting rivers."

"Poetry is very beautiful, my dear, and it's charming to be a tourist, but first men must eat."

"Eat shit?"

Silence and consternation. Philippe clears his throat. Jean-Pierre, gallant, ties it all up with his usual grace.

"You're exaggerating again, my dear, you're looking at the world through dark glasses."

Philippe clears his throat again to make the pill go down.

"My wife is really a reactionary. She calls herself progressive—am I right?" he says, turning to me, who never said any such thing, "and in reality she is a fierce reactionary. She spits on progress. She wants to spin her own clothes and make fire with two sticks. And fetch her own water—unpolluted, from the mountain spring, at dawn. Eh, my dear, wouldn't you like that?"

"I'm not against progress, I'm against crap—against using progress badly. Progress, your progress, is a kind of rape."

"Oh, oh," says Jean-Pierre, looking naughty, and Philippe: "Now really, Céline, you don't take the facts into account, you never do. . . ."

"And you two only pay attention to one kind of fact: quantity. More exactly, the quantity of money to be made in the shortest time. You think with bulldozers."

"We're in a hurry, Céline. The population is growing at a rate . . ."

"That you do everything to accelerate! Is there a

Councilor for Birth Control? I'd like to meet *him*, I have a few words to say to him!"

"That's not the point."

"It damned well is the point. It's almost the only one. And it's the one you don't come near. Taboo. France even has the distinction of being one of the two countries opposed to an international consideration of the problem. And in the meantime you are wrecking, spoiling, making everything ugly. You call it development. Shit."

"Céline, haven't I asked you . . ."

"Devastation is what you should call it. The whole planet is a slum. You have only the happiness of the people in mind, yet you make them eat poison, breathe poison, you make them live in ugliness. Beauty, there's no beauty any more."

"Beauty isn't a factor . . ." says Jean-Pierre.

"You said it, I didn't."

". . . primary factor. There are others more urgent and important to consider first."

"More important. Oh yes. *You* know what is important. You know what men are, without a sense of beauty? Much less than animals. I don't suppose you've ever observed that all there is left of dead civilizations is their beauty?"

"But are we supposed to worry about what's left after we're gone?" shouts Philippe. "We live in the present!"

"I adore the Egyptians," says Julia.

"We can't stop progress so that you can wander through a museum darling," replies her husband.

"That's a good question," I say. "My answer would be yes we can. Unfortunately there's no point asking it, because with your damned bomb there won't be any museums left."

"Here we go again," sighs Philippe, beside himself, and to the others: "Pay no attention, she's crazy."

"When the bomb comes up the world is divided into two categories: crazy men and blind ones."

"Where are you going for your vacation?" asks Philippe, to which Jean-Pierre hastens to reply that Turkey sounds very attractive to them, and we're off to the Bosphorus. "Can one visit the launching pads?" says Julia. "I would love to see how a launching pad is built," but this try doesn't go over very big, so we go off in a corner to gossip by ourselves.

As we go, Philippe says:

"Aren't you ever going to get over it?"

"I hope not, because when I do I'll be completely insensitive."

"Well, you'll have to get over it. Because I won't stand for your vile manners any more."

"Oh you were speaking of form. I thought you meant content excuse me."

"To hell with your content. All I can see is that I can't take you out with me."

"Don't take me out. For all the fun we have, I'd rather see a Western."

"The reason I have a wife is to go out with her!"

"Oh. I thought it was because you loved her."

"The two aren't mutually exclusive! Actually it should be the other way around, if you loved me you wouldn't embarrass me in public with your guttersnipe manners!"

"Oh yes. You don't mind producing shit but you don't

care to have it called by its right name when it's under your nose."

"For the last time I'm telling you . . ."

"Look, Philippe, we're alone now. But in any case, don't expect me to call it roses, prestige and prosperity."

"All right from now on the best thing is not to talk about it. It's my work, you don't have to be concerned with it, it isn't your business, it's mine."

"He's right," says Julia. "Why do you discuss it with him? What's to be gained by talking to them? They're from a different world. You have nothing to do with his business. You're his wife, not his colleague. There's only one thing for you to worry about: that he'll bring home the loot so you can spend it. Anyone would think you didn't know what marriage is, you really should begin to understand, what with all the upbringing you're getting. Let them do the talking. Be a yes-girl. Pad his dear little expense accounts. He'll be happy and you'll be happy. You're really a sucker."

Philippe likes to see me hanging out with the wives of his friends. He expects their good influence to rub off on me, unlike my past relationships, from which I drift further and further away; besides, I haven't much to say to them any more, nor they to me. . . .

Little by little, slowly, I begin. One learns, one learns. Every evening I write down the expenses of the day in a notebook; it exercises my memory and occupies my mind: toilet paper, plastic garbage can, laundry bag, while I'm doing it I can't get into mischief; at the end of the month

I add it up. When you don't keep accounts your money goes up in smoke, says Philippe, and you never know what's happened to it. But if you keep Accounts you know where you are. And it's true: where could that twenty thousand have gone? This way you know you can find it when you look for it, and if you work at it you can even find a little more. It's reassuring. You can sleep nights. Philippe cuddles up to me then and we make love. Day is done. Tomorrow another will begin at eight o'clock, with the voice of Juana telling us breakfast is served. How can we do otherwise than get up? The cups are set opposite each other, the coffee is losing its aroma, the milk is getting cold, the eggs are getting hard, and Juana is wasting time when she has so much to do, and one can't let Juana waste time when one is paying her, that would be a shame; Philippe is up, snorting and pawing the ground on the threshold of a day richly punctuated with conferences and projects, only waiting for me to get going. A whole day is waiting for me too; a house is waiting for me; I'm impeding the march of time, curled like a lazy caterpillar in our bed, which I now have all to myself, nice and warm. Well, are you getting up? I can't wait for you any more. How can I resist? Too many forces conspire against my wishful sleep.

Experience has taught me that resistance to assaults on my sleep is more harmful to it than the assaults themselves; it is true that nothing rouses the mind so much as affirming a principle; in the affirmation of the principle that it would be useless for me to get up too, my mind arms itself with agapactic wrath, and I'm already as good as up. Don't affirm anything, float: at the first call I send

my ghost to walk among them; I put myself on automatic pilot; this splendid robot, avoiding all noises and
movements which might disturb my rest, butters my toast,
dunks it carefully, sopping towards the middle of the cup
so as not to cause any accidents, toast-in-the-coffee in
particular which makes one fish it out afterwards, getting
one's fingers messy, the toast itself spongy, the butter
melted, disgusting. And the coffee greasy. Whether I'm
being a robot or not I can't stand nasty sensations like that
in the morning, it gives me a jaundiced view of life, and in
the morning I sleep with one eye closed, or even both,
but the third, inside me, is open all right, it even pulses
with life, and it is perfectly aware of its own interests,
which are the same as mine: they are to avoid all hurts,
and especially the worst the soul can sustain, which is to
experience Stupidity. In the mornings I have a soul, I
don't know what good it is, but it's mine and I must make
do with it; in the mornings, within myself, I feel warm,
pulled together, unified, true, one foot in my dreams and
one in life, if only life would show itself to me in that
luminous beauty which I see in it in the mornings. It's
not true that I'm asleep in the mornings, the truth is that
I'm not yet deadened by the unreality of the day. In the
morning I still have faith; I haven't lost it yet. In the
morning I am myself, in the morning I love myself, in the
morning I am I.

"Yes, yes."

"What do you mean yes yes? I'm asking you if we
should have the Bjebnes here to dinner or take them to a
restaurant. Yes yes is no answer."

"Just as you like, darling," murmurs the robot who guards my inner serenity.

"Not just as I like!" says my husband in a voice like a drill. "I have to know, and you have to make arrangements."

Arrangements. Brr. Beware the evil word. The robot hears the warning signal.

"Wait just a minute . . ."

"Wait for what?"

"I'm trying to remember my dream."

"Your dream! I'm talking about reality!"

Reality. The Third Eye takes note of this term with a sarcastic wink. The Robot tries delaying tactics.

"If I don't catch it now it'll disappear."

"I warn you that I'm going to disappear too. In ten minutes at the latest."

Details about time are particularly depressing. The Third Eye groans: touché. Philippe is an expert swordsman; he knows how to thrust—ten minutes to parry. I struggle desperately.

"But you'll be back."

"You mean your dreams are more important to you than I am."

"But sweetheart, I didn't say that," stammers the Robot, caught short. "I wanted to tell you because it was so beautiful. I was passing in front of a house . . ."

"Look, I have to leave in five minutes if I want to make the office on time, and with the traffic the way it is I can't even be sure of that."

"Why don't you take the métro and then you can be sure; that leaves at regular times."

"And have to decide about this dinner first."

Allusions to the métro always pass him by, which is odd, because he is so logical. "Then I heard such beautiful music coming from the house above me . . ."

". . . with the Bjebnes, whether we'll be eating out or in, and I have an appointment with the Japanese about tariffs . . ."

I was climbing a staircase with very high steps (really, Dr. Freud, didn't I get laid yesterday?) and there were red caves (better and better) and the music was getting closer and I arrived at

". . . very important meeting tomorrow right up to the time that . . ."

a great room with a black and white tile floor which I had to cross to

". . . black shoes . . ."

arrive at a kind of loggia where a light was shining behind high panes of multicolored glass

". . . Juana about starching this collar . . ."

a Venetian light, in which people were lying on furs, oh it was so beautiful! My unconscious is out of this world, a real artist. I never could have made that up myself. The question was whether I should only walk on the black tiles, or only on the white ones. A very important question, you can't deny, which symbolizes

"and tomorrow evening we have to do the tax returns."

What returns above all don't try to know. Time will tell. Too much. White tiles or black?

"last day before it's overdue. You know how much we pay for Juana?"

No, no, no! I don't want to know! I don't want to

know I don't want to! The Robot is going wild, it's in a panic, Third Eye is howling with misery. Can one stick one's fingers in one's ears when one's husband is speaking? He is saying to me—he is going to say—it is said—he said it. A number. Fatal. It's all over. The loggia, that paradise, vanishes, goes up in smoke, leaving me with my foot between the black tile and the white, not knowing what to do, I am returned to the human world, to reality as they say. Awakened, as they say. Cut off, amputated. Furious.

"Why do we have to talk about it today if it's tomorrow! Won't it already be boring enough tomorrow?"

"If I understand you correctly you're saying I bore you?"

"You're not going to tell me you think all that stuff is fun? Well, I say it's enough if just one of us is bored at a time."

"And that one has to be me?"

Oh shit.

"We all have our burdens, so I say why make this dull job a subject of conversation too? Can't we make a division of labor? All I say is that I can't see why two of us should have to be bored by the same mess at the same time, and then still keep on talking about it before we have to?"

"What's the use being married if we can't talk things over?"

"All I said was we don't have to talk about dull things."

"Being married means sharing troubles too."

"No."

"Only pleasures?"

"Yes."

"That would be convenient for you, wouldn't it, darling?"

"I didn't say that, I don't know why you can't understand me. I said it's senseless to share boring problems uselessly."

"And if I were to say you said I bore you you'd tell me you never said that?"

"What?"

He shouldn't ask so much of me at such an hour.

"What other subjects of conversation do you suggest? Huh? Go on, I'm waiting. You sit with your nose in your cup without saying a word, so I have to do all the talking."

"Why? It's nice to be quiet too."

"Thank you! I'm to shut up!"

"Anyway I wanted to tell you my dream which really was nice. It was interesting."

"To you, maybe. I'm not interested in your dreams."

"You see."

"See what?"

"You don't mind telling me *I* bore *you*. You go even farther."

"Listen to me little girl I have other things to do! besides listen to your dreams! I have realities, yes I do, to think about! While you dabble in poetry I'm busy with concrete things!"

One really can't mangle semantics to such a point, says the Third Eye, very punctilious on this question for the crack of dawn. But we're not about to start a discussion of definitions of words with such an ass.

"Well my dream disappeared, so you won!"

"Good! now you can pay some attention to what I have to say during the few seconds I have left—which I don't even have left since I'm late, thanks to you. Thanks to your dreams. Honestly! Well, I don't have the time to argue either, you're lucky. So where are we eating?"

"Restaurant." (I find that a little less sickening.)

"All right, you'll see me at eight."

"Where?"

"Didn't you hear that either?"

God knows what all I didn't hear. Aside from Black Shoes and Starched Collar I don't know a thing about this man today. Thank God he's sailing along now behind the wheel of his beautiful car not quite the most expensive but that will come when we've paid off the lease on the apartment Papa's loan taxes, sailing with his eighty horsepower at six miles an hour down the Rue de la Pompe, along with his fellow horsemen from Projects Production Committees Realizations Equipment Standing Enterprises Communications Efficiency Development Co-ordination Investment Reconversion Promotion Prosperity and New Brooms, all together shoulder to shoulder at six an hour moving on towards the Welfare of the Country via their own, if possible.

While I

While I

While I, tralala. While I loggia. I Venetian light. I music. I sleep.

The world belongs to early risers. But which world?

One of the great joys of marriage is the absence of the husband. This is something you don't know about until it happens to you. Sprawled on the couch of the spare room,

I pull my pieces together. It was my idea to have a spare room; a good idea, it makes an impression; and for whom should I have spared it if not myself? All the other rooms belong to Juana, she has reasons for going into them against which my poor reasons could never prevail. The moment the husband and wife leave the conjugal chamber she must shake out the bed linen, she must let in fresh air, the air from the Rue de la Pompe which we continue to call air for tradition's sake, tradition lives on long after reality, a couple of babies will have to be asphyxiated in front of an open window before this term is revised. But there's no need to air out the spare room, there's nothing, no pretext which can justify an intrusion—and then she gets the idea of asking me what we're going to eat today. To hell with what we're going to eat, I'm not hungry. I don't belong to Juana until eleven o'clock, an hour at which the idea of food has almost ceased to nauseate me. And haven't I had a fight to establish this rule! I had to set up a whole organization, a program! Me! I had to. A three-room establishment. And at eleven o'clock sharp, whammy! she thinks I'll be cross if she's a minute late, she arrives on the scene and I have to find something else for her to do. It's crazy how the poor soul can be thirsty for work. She can't stand ten minutes with empty hands. They must have a jolly time in her country. She gets the feeling that she's stealing her wages, God knows they're little enough; and in order to relieve her of this depressing sense of theft I have to work to find work for her, only I don't get paid for it. Is that fair? This is the other side of the coin of slavery: the master himself becomes victim to it. So I have to think of stupid things so that I can find something for her to do, and something that will be useful. The labor that I expend on finding something for the maid to do is unbelievable, I've never sweated so much for myself, I've never spent so much time on housework as since I've had help, as they say. A truly remarkable example of profit sharing. I said to her: "Read a book; or knit yourself a sweater."

"You're mad!" cries Madame Aignan. "Never tell them such things! You spoil them! Besides, it upsets them. They aren't used to it. You think you're being kind, but in fact you're doing them a disservice! She won't be grateful to you! You should do just the opposite, you shouldn't give her a minute to catch her breath, she'd be much happier. And keep after her; they find that reassuring. Believe me, I know how to handle maids."

According to Stephanie, she's run through a hundred and eighty-three of them.

"But if I've got to keep after her all the time it would be easier to do it myself—I'd do it faster. It's not worth having a maid."

"Listen, it's hard enough to find one in this day and age, you're lucky to have one, take advantage of it."

They never cease to amaze me.

"The French species is vanishing it's true," I say, more to prolong the conversation than out of any hope of convincing her, "but with the influx of slaves from the Mediterranean countries we do very well. . . ."

"Yes very true we're still lucky in that respect," says the good lady, "all the more reason to take advantage of it. Besides, Philippe should have a maid, he's used to it.

You should have seen the way he knew how to order them around even when he was a little boy."

Charming child.

"I'm sure you know how to do that sort of thing my dear child," she says, alluding delicately to my supposedly humble origins, "but Philippe would be upset."

Poor Philippe. All right at eleven o'clock to work. Stupefying activity: thinking of floor wax, or little silver spoons (why silver, it makes everything taste funny, but they're used to that). Of coppers. Think. Division of labor: one thinks, the other listens and does what she's told. Then she forgets: how is one to remember all those words? Especially when she doesn't know the language, that's the difficulty with imported slaves. So the other has to think of what she's forgotten. Viewed from the point of view of efficiency, as they like to say, it's an amazing system. Everyone has more work. Admirable. So what are we going to eat? When I was single this was something I thought about when I was hungry, I didn't ever plan it in advance. I say to Juana: Buy what looks good today. But she can't. She doesn't know whether or not what looks good to her today will look good to us today, we might decide we wanted something else, but there's no way of knowing before she's already served the thing which doesn't please us. Juana won't undertake any such responsibility, she wants to know what we want so that we can't say we don't like it later. But how are we supposed to know ourselves? So I invent; I invent things to eat out of the blue, abstractly, I take them out of my head where there really isn't anything, I have no shops in my head, so I say the first thing that comes into it, no matter what, I don't know if that will be what I want, much less what Philippe wants, if he'll want it today, later, this evening; I know nothing. So there's a sizable piece of lovely time wasted in this senseless activity, which I must renew again tomorrow and the day after and every day, and to think there are three hundred and sixty-five in a single year and one doesn't know how many years and that each day of each year the question will be asked and must be answered. One day, one of those innumerable days, I suddenly won't be able to bear asking What are we going to eat today? one more time, and necessarily I'll raise the question of Why. It's bound to happen. You go along for a long while and then it's bound to happen. It's the stupidest question in the world, but there it is, well and truly asked, and now it's too late because there's only one answer: No reason. "What shall we have for dinner today, madame?" We aren't dining today Juana, I see no reason for dining, do you? Do you see any reason for going on this way? Think about it a minute. You see. Juana rushes to the kitchen and turns on the gas. We go to a restaurant. At last, a menu!

We dine with the Bigeons and the Benoîts. Or with the Benoîts and the Duplats, or the Duplats and the Bigeons. The. They come in pairs. Couples. Or: Married Couples. Young Married; pl. "the Young Marrieds." A delicious term, you must admit. Philippe has reserved a table in one of those places where you have to reserve a table otherwise it would look as if just anybody ate there, and who is just anybody? So everybody reserves. One of those joints where they grill your steak under your nose so that you don't miss anything, sight, odor, or smoke. The next gimmick in these snooty dives, they're foolish to do it themselves, will be to let the customers cook their own grub; bent over the stove, covered with grease —they'll adore it. Nobody likes to feel closer to Nature than a bourgeois. If I opened a restaurant I'd only reserve a table if Madame agreed to come in and peel the potatoes in the morning. So you're sitting there for two solid hours because with this system the service naturally takes forever and there's always a crowd because everybody has to go to the same spots when they're in style, people are piled on top of each other and everyone yells because you have to yell to make yourself heard over the yelling of the others; you can't breathe, you get smoke poisoning, animals wouldn't stand for it they'd stampede. But we aren't animals. We stand it. That's what's called going out. After dinner it's too late to go to the movies. I would have liked to see a Western. So we go to a night club; we sit down; we order whiskies. There we are. From time to time, two of us get up and dance. We order more whiskies. Now there is cigarette smoke instead of steak smoke. My eyes burn.

My eyes never used to burn. I doubt if there was any less smoke, in all night clubs it's the same. I used to dance. Yes, honestly, I used to dance. It's when you're altogether dead that you begin to feel it. And one shouldn't go out with one's husband. It's a fact. Sad but a fact. When one is with one's husband one doesn't say the same things, one doesn't do the same things. Even Loula is less of a pain when she's alone. For my part, even if he just goes out to the can I immediately begin to sparkle; when he comes back I fade again. Why? A supernatural phenomenon. Do you suppose men are under the same spell? It would be nice to think so; that would allow us to hope that there is more to them than meets our eye. But the strangest thing is why we insist on clinging together when it produces such a constipating effect. Weird custom. Why, why? Why? I'm new to the scene; I look around with a fresh eye. Everything still amazes me. The others don't seem to realize. They chatter on about a thousand subjects. Films, plays, cars, other people. Then the smoke begins to burn my eyes. Burn and burn. The whisky is bitter. It makes me thirsty. The sparkling water makes me thirsty. The lemonade makes me thirsty. I smoke my cigarettes down to the last quarter inch. The cigarette makes me thirsty. Or else we play bridge with some of the Young Marrieds. Ice whisky soda water cigarettes. Thirst. I play terrible bridge. When we began I went through a period of brilliance, Philippe was enchanted, at last there's something she knows how to do. And then I began to play terribly, I forgot what cards had been played, what was trump, who had bid, and I played against my partner; I loved to be dummy. I can only go so far. After bridge, we play poker if we're in the mood. Everybody thinks I'm a rotten player—I play a weird game they say to be polite. I confuse the game, I break things up, I prevent them from playing Good Poker. That may be but every time I'm the one who walks off with the pot. They aren't happy about it; to lose their money to such a bad player upsets them. But that's the only part that interests me, taking their loot; I'll do any-

73

thing to attain that objective; I'd cheat if I knew how; I want their dough. Since I have to sit there dying of boredom, it seems to me they ought to pay for it. They want to play Good Poker. For Art's sake. I say to hell with poker I want to win their money; and I do.

"Do you really love money?" says Philippe, though he's really rather pleased by this characteristic in me. "If the game reveals true character, and I think it does, my God, you really love money, Céline!"

"That depends on which money."

"It can't depend on which money. Money is money."

At any rate I finally paid for my pants with that money; I've always lived from hand to mouth as Philippe says; and not just any old pair, a beauty, a sort of cobalt blue, in stretch silk, a knockout, and Philippe had nothing to say about it, it didn't show up in the accounts. So I have my little pleasures after all. Naturally I can't wear them when we're "going out." When we go out the little wives are all dressed more or less alike. Except for me, because I don't have my stole yet. But I'm still a beginner.

"You'll get one," says Julia. "If you start working on it now you'll have it by Christmas of next year. In his position Philippe can't wait too long for his wife to get her mink, it would cause talk."

"To hell with mink I don't want it."

"Come on now don't say that; don't be unreasonable. There are lots of nice things about mink, it's light it's warm it's pretty it's becoming to everybody, and it wears well. It can last longer than the marriage, in some cases."

When Julia's around life is bearable. She's a real pro. She got married because she doesn't know how to do a damned thing and she's lazy. I like her; she knows the score. I like people who know the score whatever it is. All in all, considering what each of us is like, and we're quite different, she's much less of a babe in the woods than I am.

"Why didn't you become a whore?"

"Too tiring. Always having to go upstairs. And then do you realize how many times a day it would come to? With Jean-Pierre it's only once or twice a week. If it's just one man you can put up with it."

"Don't you like men?"

"Show me one and I'll let you know. With the ones we've got," she says, surveying the field, "how do you expect me to feel?"

It's true. The last time I saw any was during our Honeymoon Trip I think. Usually they were herding cattle. Not that I have a perverse taste for the noble savage, but you have to admit that virility seems to be in inverse proportion to urbanization, however stupid, inconvenient and illogical that may be. Anyway, I did see some men then; I even remarked on it to Philippe. In those days I believed in Sincerity in Marriage. I made a completely ordinary comment about a guy on a horse; the horse was just as good as he was and I think I compared them. You couldn't say I went overboard. Besides which we were in a car doing eighty, tourist speed. But Philippe didn't like it.

"If you can't control yourself at least wait until I'm not around. It would show more delicacy."

"But Philippe . . . you can hardly say I'm throwing

myself at him! I'm not even thinking of it! At this speed it wouldn't be easy, since I'm not a cowboy."

He didn't like the joke either, he found it vulgar. He has a horror of vulgarity. Between the thought and the deed, he observed, there is very little difference. Only opportunity. "Isn't that true?" says Philippe. "Honestly?"

To be honest, obviously if the circumstances were right, if I were alone, unmarried, idle, for instance if the car had broken down, and the horse too, I wouldn't make any promises. It's the best way to get to know a country; I know that much about trips. Not honeymoon trips, to be sure. But as Philippe says, it's all a matter of opportunity. However, between the accomplished and the unaccomplished fact there is just the difference that nothing *has* happened, I thought it would be all right to mention it.

"So we can't talk about it?"

Maybe that's what the characters do in the books I read (he imagines I do the most amazing reading, I wish I knew the titles of the books). But it's pretty far-out stuff (titles, titles!). "And since you insist on pursuing the subject, there is only one fidelity, and that is not even to have the idea of straying."

Yes that's true. It says so in the Bible. I sink into meditation. Philippe is strong-minded. He's obsessed with the Absolute the way some people are with golf. To such a point that you'd have to be perfect to meet his standards. I wonder if he's thought of how this applies to himself. But he's in luck; it's not the kind of problem which is likely to become pressing here in this city, in this group, as Julia says in her own way. The types that we hang out with, the gray flannel boys, rats in the race of Industry and the State, are not likely to arouse irrepressible passions. What kind of trouble can you get into with a Jean-Pierre Bigeon, an Hervé Benoît? They're about as animated as lampposts. A dog could pee on their legs, but a woman couldn't dream about them at night; although the dear souls always behave as if they were confident of the opposite, which makes us die laughing. As Philippe says, in our circle one doesn't even think of such things, and except for suffering from a chronic bovarysm which is endemic though in my case I came to marriage without frustration no one has much trouble being faithful. I am. Obedient to Philippe's scriptural principles I don't so much as raise my eyes to them, it's as if they didn't exist. If Philippe weren't beginning to take on certain resemblances to them as time passes, there would be nothing to worry about.

But Philippe is satisfied on the whole. To have taken a slut like me, whom he found in the gutter, or at a party which is the same thing, and to have successfully made me into a faithful wife is a triumph which he attributes entirely to his own merits, including that of satisfying me daily . . . except on those three days when a woman is impure; that is it's four days at the moment and I have a feeling it's going up to five. That's how it is. I couldn't say why. Just life, I guess.

"You can get away with six or seven without their catching on, plus migraine the day before and resting up the day after," says Julia. "They think of us as delicate children; it doesn't surprise them; I think they like it."

"I'm not so sure about Philippe. He wants it every day."

"You've trained him badly."

"I couldn't help it. I was in love. Anyway I wasn't going to deprive myself. And I think that's his nature—after all it's more or less a virtue."

"It's yours too, if I understand you."

"I don't know. I'm not the type who gives it up for Lent that's for sure. My goodness, it's fun to make love, don't you think so?"

"Oh I'm half frigid you know."

"That's terrible! You should see a doctor! A psychoanalyst! You can't go on like that you poor thing! Tell me about your life and I'll straighten you out it only takes a little common sense. Then you can put the psychiatrist's fees in the household accounts and you'll make some money . . ."

"Oh don't bother there's no mystery; one day I just lost my energy. At first everything was all right, as soon as I'd found one who wasn't too clumsy. And then one day I just suddenly got lazy. There really isn't anything to talk about. I think I just got too bored with it. I lost my enthusiasm."

"Of course, if you're bored. You have to feel inspired to get pleasure out of it. We aren't machines."

"Inspired! You're a scream. Have you found men who inspired you?"

"Not around here obviously. Except for Philippe: he's my first bourgeois. But other places sometimes. Mainly in foreign countries. Anyway, I have found some. I suppose in most cases I mistook a firefly for a light bulb. But I wanted them to be light bulbs so badly! Lighthouses! I'd go after the slightest glow, always hopeful. It was usually an optical illusion, as I'd realize later. But while I believe in it, it seems like a miracle."

"That's all right if you can count on your imagination. But I have no imagination. I see what I see."

"Maybe. But not entirely. It's not all imagination. There's something somewhere that's real. Just a tiny crumb here and there. Very tiny. Maybe we should be grateful just for that. Maybe life is made up of tiny crumbs. Perfection is for heaven."

"So now you believe in God?"

"No, but I'm trying to express what I mean in recognizable terms. What if crumbs are all there is? maybe that's the way you have to accept it, and I don't know how. Of course I don't know how, I'm not Confucius! I always start out believing that the thing's perfect. Maybe you need that illusion; anyway it helps. For me other things are all mixed up in it, too: the landscape, the weather, a song that's being played at the time. They all go together to make a whole. It's mysterious. Once I made love with the moon."

"You may be just plain crazy."

"Could be. But look at you, you're frigid and I'm not, so who's crazy? Anyway, I'm not crazy, I'm right: the moon is beautiful. Anyone who doesn't know that is crazy."

"What does that make Philippe? The planet Mars?"

"I don't give a damn. It was dawn; he took me away from a wild party, put me in his car, and had me in a meadow . . ."

"Did he think you were a cow?"

"The sun was rising."

"I see."

"The air was fresh and pure."

"The lure of the open road."

"The road to Carmel."

"What?"

"Carmel and Damascus combined. He said: This is more like it, eh? He meant better than the place we'd left; he hadn't taken his eyes off me all evening. He said: Do you really like all that? he meant all that debauchery. 'In your heart of hearts, does it satisfy you?!' In my heart of hearts, at dawn, drunk what do you think? He asked me: 'Are you happy the way things are?'"

"And now are you happy?" says Julia.

ONE ACCEPTS an invitation to bliss, to rapture; one wakes up a housekeeper. In a Carmel too it's true that one is given humble tasks which one must accept with a joyous heart for the greater glory of God. Amen.

And as God is my witness, I've been good as gold. I've done everything he wanted. I've obeyed orders precisely. If I got a bit stubborn at times, during the early period of adjustment, I always gave in at the end. Now I don't fight any more. Whatever it is, I do it. Let him who is without sin cast the first stone. What he wants, he gets. Whatever he expects of a Real woman, from Absolute Love, he has it. His socks are washed. His collars are, or are not starched. His black shoes are blacked. There are no spots on his suits. The toilet paper is replenished according to his needs. The table is set when he gets home. The accounts are balanced. I get up with him and discuss the schedule for the day. Every day the menu takes into account his Metabolism and tastes. I give dinners. My table is renowned: since I wasn't raised as a bourgeoise, I know what good food is; when I feed people, I feed them, they can hardly drag themselves around afterwards, and the next day they have liver attacks. I have taught Juana French cooking, for which purpose I took the trouble to learn Spanish so now I can speak it, a good deed is never a total loss and when I give orders I really sound elegant. Also I take pains, which always pays off; for example when I have a Belgian to dinner I never forget to have potatoes as well as green vegetables on the table, if it's an Italian he'll get his Parmesan and his toothpicks, etc.; Philippe entertains a great many visitors from neighboring countries, Benelux Common Market and Tutti Quanti. As for old friends, I'm careful to remember their likes and dislikes, and if I make a mistake it's always on purpose.

The In-Laws have forgotten their doubts. I call them Mother and Father at least three times in each sentence; I do nothing by halves, which is the only way to find happiness, the only inner happiness there is lies in doing things wholeheartedly. I chatter: I say yes yes indeed. I put ashtrays beside each chair, I light cigarettes (very much appreciated), not one gets by me, out comes a cigarette and hop! there I am with my flaming lighter. I think by now I could draw a six-shooter as fast as a gun slinger. I have all the dishes offered three times, always very full (the quantity of food we throw away in this joint is a scandal; I'd have a public soup kitchen at my back door if I had a little heart). I watch over everyone's glass being filled, never an empty one if I can see it, I have a bar almost as good as Harry's, I pour it into my clients as if they were goatskins, a regular little geisha. No half measures. I don't just serve olives with the apéritifs, but several kinds of sausage, shrimp with finger bowls, and when I'm really swinging, caviar. Philippe has his doubts about all this, but then people are so obviously impressed that he is consoled. Sometimes I have candles burning; they drip they smell they flicker but people do love to be reminded of the good old days. And on my fine damask tablecloths I serve hash *à l'Auvergne* and mutton stew with lima beans, which they won't often find elsewhere. Stew by candlelight is chic. They like it. While they stuff themselves the record player serves them preselected music, Suite for Royal Diners which is really the least one can do or the Unfinished Symphony, with a record that gets in by mistake sometimes, Mingus or Kurt Weill or a bawdy ballad, once it was the International which really put the damper on things. Afterwards they have a choice of whisky of every nationality. The whole thing must be perfect or it isn't worth the effort. I go from one guest to another, I circulate; I never stop. What would I do if I did stop? At least this way I'm busy, time passes, the evening is over, finally.

At the end I feel a healthy physical fatigue, especially in my feet from standing on them so long. Philippe takes me in his arms, he is happy, he repeats all the compliments he has received on his charming wife, and God knows they go right to my heart: I have exquisite taste, delightful ideas, I take so much trouble, I see that everything goes well. How rare is a virtuous woman! Her husband has entrusted her with his heart. She does good, not evil unto him. All the days of her life. Her work is done in gladness. She is like a rich merchant ship, her husband is welcomed in all ports. She is clothed in power and glory, and she laughs at the future. . . .

. . . Grace is a mockery, and beauty is vain.

Philippe feels our entertaining in his pocket, I don't stint on it, but it pays off. It's not an expense it's an investment. And anyway, his money is never really lost when he can find it in the account book, all written down, candles included.

I don't say shit in public any more. What's the use? In general I talk very little, I don't express my ideas; in fact I don't have any. I am polite amiable sweet— How sweet your wife is! I'm not exactly scintillating, of course, but you can't have everything. And it doesn't really matter, there are plenty of others to do the talking. I've lost the habit; one loses it fast. I listen, I listen, how can I explain it? with my third ear. All of sudden I've developed one. I don't listen to what they say (which is never of the slightest, slightest, slightest interest) but to how they say it. The rhythm. The sound. It's funny. Much more interesting. Let's say one says: White (the subject doesn't matter—a film, the Russians—that's not the point); the other says: Black. White speaks. Black waits; not for the end, but for a gap to rush into with his reply. White doesn't listen: he watches Black so as not to miss the moment when Black leaves his gap, whether it's when he lights his cigarette or takes a swallow of his drink, then White can throw himself into the breach and begin to talk once more; then he listens to himself attentively while Black waits. Often there are several of them in the free-for-all, they dash into the pauses all together and twitter like sparrows until one comes out on top. And all their sentences begin: Personally *I* . . .

Example: "Personally I find that the Victory is the best car on the market," says Jean-Pierre Bigeon, who never talks about anything else. "The transmission . . ." (for more exact details see the company prospectus). Because the funny thing is that once they've said *Personally I*, they repeat what they've picked up from someone else word for word—content, syntax, and vocabulary. The only thing which is personal is the combination *PersonallyI*, the rest is pure repetition. Any original thought is contained in that *PersonallyI*, any human emotion. The rest is not worth listening to, not the words, what one must really hear is the sound: it's all nervous and strangled, as if they were being choked; it has no body to it; sometimes they give such loud yelps that animals would run away if they heard them. But since no one is listening no one runs away. If the others were listening to the sound instead of waiting desperately to take the floor, they would undoubtedly hear the same things that I do, they couldn't help it unless they were deaf, and afterwards they'd avoid such a hornet's nest. I can't get into it any more. It's over for me. I've removed myself a little, oh not much, I don't appear to have moved at all, but that little move is insuperable all the same. A pane of glass separates me from them. I don't know quite what made it: I guess I produced it by that little imperceptible movement of retreat; since then they've been in an aquarium.

I remember as if from a prenatal world the time when I used to get involved with them, leaving myself open to anger and empty insults. I couldn't do it any more if I wanted to. They have become like images on a screen, and their words reach me like the voices of dolphins on another wave length. Two disconnected worlds: in one, a hypnotic trance, in the other, waking. If you judge by appearances, body movements, the excitement in voices, they are the ones who are awake, while I, mute and motionless, must be sleeping. And sometimes I feel as if I were asleep. I think that I've become schizophrenic. But God in heaven, it is they who are the true madmen!

But at least I'm left in peace this way; if someone speaks to me I simply answer Yes yes; that's all right, they never listen anyway. Who cares about my opinions? What do I care about them myself? I can live without them. I don't even think I have any any more. Blah blah blah. How many lumps of sugar do you take. They're satisfied. Philippe is satisfied.

Actually, everything is not quite perfect yet. I still hate doing the joint income tax; I don't answer letters promptly, I forget birthday cards and some bills; I don't remember to buy little things He needs, I don't file Household papers in the file reserved for this purpose, with compartments, that He bought just to make things easier for me, I still have shortcomings, still make omissions, which, since they happen too often, annoy Him, He is obliged to comment on them which is tiring for Him who already has so much to do—but I'm getting there little by little, this too shall pass, eventually I'll take care of it; like the rest.

I really am getting terribly well organized. I even have some time to myself. Fine, but what am I supposed to do

with it? I don't know. I open the door to the spare room.
It is empty.

I don't dream any more. Or maybe I just don't remember that I do? I'm always wide awake. I think I've lost
my unconscious. I call: no echo. I survey the apartment,
living room, four other rooms and closets, I look to see if
anything is out of place. I inspect. Guest room, no guest.
I close the door softly. I don't make any noise. I don't like
noise. The mirrors give back my reflection as I move
through the hallway: who is that? I don't like that lady
passing by me, her pale smooth face is a pool of emptiness.
I turn from her. I don't want to meet her. Madame, accept my sincere best wishes. Run away. Read, but what?
"La chair est triste hélas"—oh no, that's by someone I
can't stand. Couldn't stand. I don't know who any more.
I only remember I couldn't stand him and especially not
that sentence. That sentence is not for me. Who is me?
Me—now goes to sleep over the first page of a book;
after all it's only printed words. The telephone rouses me,
it's Loula, who has found a new masseur, fantastic touch,
it's Elizabeth, her kid has measles, it's Minou, would I
like to go to a marvelous fortuneteller with her? I go, I
love fortunetellers, they say such wild things: I can't See
you very clearly. . . . It's strange. . . . You don't seem
to want to emerge . . . your cards are a blank. . . . I see
absolutely Nothing. Or it's Our Mother who is giving a
tea, there's always that. On Thursday it's Stephanie, she
wants to see a Mickey Mouse, that's great; but there's
only one Thursday a week, and then it seems to me I'm
disappointing Stephanie, I think she expects something of
me I can't give, I think I bore her somehow. No, I don't

get drunk any more; whisky doesn't taste good to me; the brand I used to like seems to have disappeared from the market without my noticing. When I drink I just fall asleep. Is it only four o'clock? I thought it was six and time for Philippe to come home, this evening we're having a dinner party, what shall I wear? that's a good subject to think about, but it's too early still. Play a record. But which. Which. Let's see. You have to want music. You don't just listen to any music that's around because you've decided. It's not just a time killer. I've tried that way, but it's no longer music, just sound. In school I learned that music is only vibrations in the air, and it's very true.

I remember the time I played that Sinfonia of Vivaldi's six times in succession, the one with the scratch in the middle of the record. And Matthew's Passion. And my fervor for the Spanish Civil War songs! I played them over and over. Music is funny. You get wild crazes. During that period I wore out a record a week. Where are the passions of yesteryear? In this house we take good care of our records. They're in a closed cabinet. Because of dust. It's true that dust is bad for records, and naturally things are made to be preserved rather than used. But try to find a record in a cabinet! You have to open it, etc. Records should be where you can get at them. Where are my old ones? Arranged alphabetically with the rest. I ought to separate them so that I can find them when I want them. But how can I find my old passions? None of it means anything any more, yet they're all there. Archive Collection complete works of. Just seeing the name of Beethoven kills me, and in this damned barracks there are a lot of long-plays with several composers on the same side;

that makes me so furious I'd break them—if they weren't unbreakable, this junk. All you can do is bend them. They belong to Philippe, of course, the ones with several composers. But why shouldn't manufacturers collect several composers on a record when there are plenty of jerks around to buy them? You can't expect manufacturers to be saints. Calm down, baby, or you'll have a headache this evening. Every time I lose my temper I get a headache in the evening, the doctor warned me about it. I have pills to calm me down and pills to pep me up, so that the calming ones won't calm me down too much. And a few more so that the others won't damage my liver. It seems I have a liver now. Like Philippe. The doctor discovered it. Philippe is triumphant; he was sure I did, despite my denials. Considering the life I'd been leading. Now I lead a normal life. They dose me for it.

And am I happy this way? Philippe doesn't ask these days.

So what is there to do? If you're happy, I can't see anything left to do. You're happy and that's it. That's it. That's it. That's it. That's it. . . . I have everything I need. First of all, I have him, Himself. I even have my mink. And not just a stole, if you please, a whole coat. Let's be honest, on me it looks good. The others adore it, I saw it in their faces, and an all-out offensive began among the Young Marrieds.

Wedding Anniversary. Fur Wedding. The furriers should introduce the idea I know it would be a huge success, I'm going to patent the idea. They already have an obligatory Christmas, Mothers' Day, Fathers' Day, but there's room for more. Now, according to Julia, I should get my pearls soon. Pearl Wedding.

Oh but I've been so good, so good! I deserve the best. I haven't looked at a man since I was married, at least not since the guy on the horse; who can say more? Not a single man. Not a gesture, not a direct look; just out of the corner of my eye. I'm like an iceberg. I simply don't think about men. I'm out of the habit. I don't know what it's like any more. Even if you discount the fact that what's available is not what you'd call tempting—because other people make do with what's available, and if I'd really been looking I'm sure I would have seen one or two, in other neighborhoods, on the streets. I haven't looked. I don't want to. I just don't give a damn. I'm dead inside, there's no excitement, my temperature doesn't rise, nothing. I don't even understand the dirty stories the men tell after dinner now; it's true I never pay attention to what they're saying, but I can tell by the sound of their voices (more vulgar, though still depthless) that they are telling dirty stories. And I must say I don't think they ought to, men like that who take such a high moral tone about everything else, they oughtn't to say such things in front of the ladies, who are frail creatures, after all, and subject to temptation. Not me though. I have nothing between my legs. It's gone, flown away little bird, bye-bye. Maybe I'm finished?

The other day I saw a couple kissing in the métro. On the mouth. You could see everything. I even thought you could see too much, I was shocked. I asked myself, Why are they doing that, what do they see in it? No use re-minding myself that I myself, here in this very métro, had done the same thing, no question about it, just as immodestly, and with just such passion and indifference to everybody around me, I don't remember with whom any more but I did it, and this present lack of understanding of mine is really queer, I have no right—but I can't help it, I couldn't imagine what anyone saw in it any more. I'm ashamed to admit it but it even seemed disgusting to me, those mingled mouths. I told myself it must be age, I'll soon be thirty, and now I'll have to be careful not to turn into an old biddy, to try to stay liberal, to be understanding with the young. Really, I'm through with being kissed on the mouth, it's something I don't understand any more. And to desire a man! My reputation is now established. I'm the faithful Madame Aignan. Philippe can carry his hornless head high, without inviting the ridicule we heap upon Jean-Marc or Hervé, or even Jean-Pierre, whom Julia deceived once just on principle. I don't even have any principles. I have exactly nothing. Some of them were stupid enough to try something with me, affording me a splendid occasion to embroider on the theme Have you taken a good look at yourself lately? which I'd been longing to do for some time. They're marvelous. So tactful! and modest! They say: "A woman" can't always be faithful, come on, you aren't made of wood, are you? "A woman" can't hold out forever. And I: That depends on who she's holding out on. From a real man, maybe not; but from you! Look, "Have you taken a good look at yourself lately?" You think a person could look at you and think about sex? People think about stock market reports when they look at you, my friend! I even took Jean-Pierre, who was getting all excited (Why? I'm not exciting these days, and I know what being excited means. Have they made a bet among themselves that the proud Philippe who probably bores them to death in those conversations they have, with his beautiful conjugal security, and his *When it comes to women I know how to manage them, etc.* that even he can be reduced to their level?), I even took Jean-Pierre up to a full-length mirror and gave him a real going over. Since I had the inside story on certain things which don't show up in mirrors (when we girls get together our conversation is more scientific than poetic) I landed a few low blows in the form of questions which didn't give away my sources. After that his manliness left him as can be imagined. When I'd made him admit that it was for a bet, I told him that the only reason I wasn't unfaithful to Philippe was that there were no real men around. Every man should know his place. And it gave me a great deal more pleasure than if I'd said yes. As for Hervé since he's an ass I made a date to meet him in a bar near the Madeleine just two steps from the houses of assignation where he was already picturing himself making out with me triumphantly, and I sent Philippe there to show him how loyal his old friend Benoît was. They don't see each other any more and that rid me of Loula at the same time, I was getting pretty sick of her two-hour phone calls and her masseurs and her three brats. You should never pass up the chance to have some fun there aren't so many of them.

I never squealed on Jean-Pierre. Not that he wasn't shitty too, but I'm fond of Julia. Of course I told her everything, we always discuss things like that. We talk about men for hours, not from the point of view of senti-ment; nor of dirt either. Let's say we make an analysis of their behavior, precise and scientific. I'm planning to write a Dissertation. Once I took some courses in Ethnology, but they disappointed me a little. There were gaps in the curriculum. It set out to examine the customs of savage peoples, but it never touched on the Race called White. Called Civilized. Called "developed"; haha. I think I'll de-vote myself to this cause. I'll be the Malinowski of the Occidental World. It's an unexplored area which has need of one. Because it isn't fair that just by opening a book the whole world has an opportunity of finding out how the gallant Melanesians make love, but the procedure of the White Occidental can only be found in the *Memoirs* of Casanova and the boasting of drunks; and these only tell about quantity, a phenomenon of no interest, omitting the qualitative aspect, which seems to be an unknown con-cept here. I'm competent to do it, I've examined enough specimens at close range, *in vivo*. Between Julia and me there's an appreciable body of observation, at least equal to the samplings from which most experts work. If need be, we'll add some serious investigations, for which we have good tests. I take notes. We have fun. With Julia, I feel alive again. One day I even came to life again. It was hot we'd just taken a shower, undisturbed no one at home. We wanted to give each other pleasure. We did. Simply. Like that. For pleasure.

Isn't that nicer than doing it alone? And so much more satisfying.

Good God. I'd forgotten how it felt.

I looked at myself in the mirror. I knew myself at once. There I am, that one, there! I! I! Where had I been? Where had I disappeared to? Who's that other female pacing the rooms of the apartment in the Rue de la Pompe?

It is Madame Philippe Aignan.

W<small>E WERE GOING</small> on vacation the following week, each household separately. In one way it was a good thing: we were getting a taste for it. We were always shopping in the stores together, dresses to be fitted, so-called putting things in order, obviously it's necessary to make all sorts of preparations before a vacation, there's a lot of work. Huge activity reigned in the two households, the husbands viewed it all with tenderness. And in the evening, the wives came home in such a good mood. It was so funny to do that to them. "I spent the afternoon with Julia." That's no lie!

I'm off, full of fire and life. Oh, there's still a little something missing, but I feel alive. I sing. How long has it been since I sang? Philippe looks at me with surprise; he's never heard me before, it seems I have a voice. It's a beautiful day. Philippe is happy too, for other reasons; his 508 hard top that he's been waiting for since the automobile show has been delivered, all the advantages of a sports car and none of the inconveniences, four adjustable seats, you can sleep in it without having a trailer (thank God) automatic sprinklers four compartments air conditioning artificial respiration musical glove storage safety belts elevator for all I know lots of chrome and besides that it goes. Philippe's joy is doubled by the fact that Jean-Pierre hasn't yet got his Victory de luxe sports car 220 kilometers an hour thousand horsepower excuse me if I've got the details wrong but he's given us such a dose of it that it's understandable if I'm confused. In the meantime, Philippe is Prince of the Road in his. Not many people have this model yet, we've only met one other in five hundred kilometers and it put his nose out of joint for a while. In a moment of overconfidence, or else because I'm brainwashed by hearing it praised from the moment of departure, I'm not made of wood, I ask if I can drive it.

It's been a long time since I've been so daring. Not since the time I stripped the gears in the old one, I was used to Thomas' English car where they go the other way. After that I didn't try again because I saw how it hurt him, poor darling. But today I'm in high spirits.

"No. You'll ruin it. A new car."

Second try:

"It's still being broken in."

He's lying, he broke it in on the turnpike before we left.

"Fifteen hundred miles is enough."

"Not for a car like this."

"But I know about breaking it in, you don't have to be a magician."

"You have to get the feel of the motor. You aren't used to it."

"And this way I'll never get used to it."

"I'm not interested in your getting used to it in my car. Thanks a lot."

Fifteen hundred. Seventeen hundred. How broken in can it get?

"Okay then, buy me one."

"I thought you looked down on cars."

I look down on men who talk about them. Naturally he mixes it up on purpose. Eighteen hundred. He's stalling, he's stalling.

"I won't go fast."

"So we'll lose time?"

"But we have plenty of time!"

"That's no reason."

Two thousand. If this were an atomic plant I could see why he wouldn't want me to touch it. But it's a plain old car. Even if the worst happened, it could be fixed.

"You talk so much about how well built it is, I should think it could withstand my driving."

"Céline, what's the matter with you? I've never seen you so contrary."

"Contrary, for once I want something. That doesn't happen very often."

Two thousand one hundred, two hundred, two-fifty.

"Let me drive, Philippe."

"You're being stubborn."

"Stubborn! I like that! I want to drive and I'm not allowed, so I'm supposed to forget about it. I warn you, I'm not going to forget about it."

"Ha!"

He seems to have run out of arguments. I began to whine.

"I used to drive. I haven't driven since my wedding. I'll get so I don't know how any more. It's ridiculous."

"Did you bring your license?"

"Certainly."

"Oh. You brought it."

He's frankly disappointed.

"You could break a leg. You never can tell, huh? It happens sometimes, doesn't it? Then you'd really be in a spot. And I'm used to driving at night I have very good eyes and you don't like to. Suppose we had to drive at night? And you were tired? Or you were sick? Or if . . ."

He gives in. He can't fight any more. He sees I can keep this up for the whole trip. And I would have kept up, I'd decided to annoy him. I'm really fed up. There's no reason for it. The car belongs to me too, we're married (excuse me, we're married under the rule of separate property so nothing can be mine, I hadn't thought of that, boy, they've got it made. But just the same there's no reason for it).

"Let's see how you do, then!" he says, regretfully but with condescension. To hell with him. I'm off. Oh, it's nice. It's a beautiful day. I've always loved to drive. I'd forgotten that, too.

"Watch it!"

There he is beside me, completely rigid, his right hand gripping the door, his left tensed to grab the steering wheel. I feel it.

"You're going too fast— Look out— On your left."

"What?"

"That guy's going to pass you."

"I see him. Let him pass."

"Don't speed up then!"

"I'm not speeding up."

"Yes you are. Céline, you aren't going straight. Look ahead of you—don't look at the hood."

"I'm not looking at the hood."

"Yes, you are looking at the hood! Third, third, I said, pass in third! —Bear right, you're in the middle of the road! Oh, oh, Céline, watch out for the guy on the bicycle, you nearly shaved his behind!"

"What bicycle?"

That's to put him in his place. The crap he expects me to put up with, really the crap!

"My God, Céline, you're going to kill us! Céline, you're going to kill us! The truck! The truck Céline! Oh! Céline, stop! Stop, I can't stand it! Stop! No, not there! You can't stop in the middle of the road! Go on farther but slowly please! slowly. Use your signal. Pass in second. In second."

Where is second? I don't know any more. Shit shit shit shit!

"There. Go there. But watch out for the tree. Now. The brake. God!"

He's completely shaken up, he's pale, he's trembling.

"Get out, hurry up."

I get out. But I don't know if I'll get in again. I'm really undecided about it.

"Well, what are you waiting for? Get in! What are you waiting for?"

What can I do out here in the middle of nowhere? I'd have to get my suitcase, and what would I do with a suitcase if I were hitchhiking? I hate having anything to carry. And besides, I want to go where the sun is shining. As for hitchhiking, here's somebody telling me to get in and my suitcase is already in the car. I get in—for practical reasons. Weakly. He goes off like a shot. There he is, he's holding it, he has it, he got it back, he's happy. Reassured. I hear him sigh deeply.

"My poor baby, you're not exactly talented."

"All right let's not go over it it isn't worth it it's over."

"What's over?"

"Whatever you wanted."

"And what is it I wanted according to you?"

"To make me feel small."

"As if I could! Haha!"

"I told you it's all right. Keep your toy. Just try not to kill me, I'm fond of my skin. That's all I'm asking. Because just between the two of us I've seen better drivers than you though I haven't mentioned it before."

"Haha, sour grapes."

"Keep your eyes on the road."

I could pay him back in kind, but it isn't worth the trouble. And as I said, I'm fond of my skin, and that kind of joke can be fatal. It's an unbreakable rule that you shouldn't drive with your husband beside you. There should be a law against it; it's dangerous. Even Fangio would run into a tree if he had somebody beside him positively wetting his pants all the time.

What a bastard. No one can mistrust you, no one can rob you of self-confidence like a husband. It took mine two tries but in the end he's won, I won't dare touch a wheel again. I was weaving all over the road at the end, and I didn't know which pedal was the clutch any more, it was awful. A public menace. And to think I used to be known as the expert at ten-hour night runs. Philippe is worn out by six, we have to stop. How I used to drive my sleeping or drunken pals around the roads of the Côte d'Azur in the small hours of the morning! I loved that, when they were all sleeping and I was the only one awake, the stars flying by overhead. Oh yes, I did like that! That's what cars are for. To have fun, with friends; taking side roads. Just to drive along the turnpike this way is drudgery, when I had to do it for my pals I thought of it as a job I did in exchange for the price of the trip. Anyone with any sense would know it's work, and would get paid for it. It should be assigned to professionals, like locomotive engineers. At least with an engineer in the locomotive you dare to relax! They're qualified and they know they have a responsibility. While a private driver! You think he's responsible? Look at him: Monsieur at the wheel, seeing nothing of the countryside, filled with pride because his speedometer is at one hundred fifty as if he deserved credit because the machine was specifically designed for this purpose and all he has to do is press down his foot. We must be crazy to put up with it; a fellow who'd lost his sense of reality to such a point in any other area would be thrown in the clink; drunk with power on that inch of space, masturbating with the sole of his foot, people have been put in strait jackets for less. And my life is in the hands of this maniac; I must be crazy too now that I think of it.

At last, as a reward for his efforts, we're getting closer to the sun, and with a little luck we'll get there. I sit back in my corner. I look at the countryside since I have the time to look at it, or at least as much of it as I can see. From time to time I give a little cry of fright and grip the seat, so he won't enjoy life too much. I daydream. I think sexy thoughts about recent events. While my chauffeur toils away.

I want sun. Sun sun. Completely stupefied, stunned by the sun like an animal without thought I shall drift through this vacation. I lie on the boat stripped to the buff, so I won't have any strap marks I say, I'm drowning in sun. Since Philippe is buying me some sunshine, I must take advantage of it I want every bit of it I want it all over. I'd want it inside if I could have it there. It's a real idyll, he ought to be jealous. I have an elemental passion, physical, monstrous, for the sun. I must have a sickness which only the sun can cure. In the evening when it has set I want to dance. I've already missed out on two new dances since my marriage and there's another new one beginning. They're really fabulous. I have to catch up on them. To miss new dances is to grow old. To miss out on the latest thing, to stop, to be out of step: to grow old.

"I feel like a fool carrying on that way," says Philippe.

No, no, look, you have to throw yourself into it. I insist, I try to keep him on the beat while he lumbers like a bear opposite me.

"And you look like a fool too. We look like two fools."

An old couple. Old marrieds. Sitting at our table now, dignified, watching the young people enjoy themselves as befits their age. Thirty. Thirty. It tolls like a knell. Thirty.

Maybe he's right, you shouldn't try to stay on the train past your stop, it's "foolish." I could cry. I see them really swinging out there. What a good time they're having! How happy they are! I'm sick with envy. I don't want to get old! Not me, I don't want to!

You're hysterical, my girl, says a severe inner voice which has the sound of mine but the tone of Philippe's. Hysterical. You're a has-been, poor thing. Think of those young people yesterday, playing volley ball, how you threw yourself at the ones who needed a player; it's a sign; the taste for youth. Don't butt in that way, says Philippe. But they called me! I make them laugh! Obviously, if you play the clown to ingratiate yourself. Are you playing with your kindergarten again? says Philippe. Oh, all right. There's always the sun. The sun belongs to everybody, even me. Philippe covers me, and points at some boats about five hundred meters away: Put your clothes on. Finally I got sunburned when I thought I was past the risk. There you are, you always go too far, you have no idea of what your limits are.

Isn't it funny how nasty he is all of a sudden? I've been "limiting" myself for an age and he never noticed. But the minute I stick my neck out a little he chops off my head. When you don't need him he's right there, Philippe. As for knowing one's limits, he knows his. He takes care of himself, that kid. He watches his step. I thought he was in better shape. In the beginning that was what impressed me, he seemed to be in such good shape; an oak, I used to say, solid as an oak. Those big, well-built blond boys, you think they're like rocks when you look at them but in fact they're delicate as little girls. Effort exhausts them; if they don't get their sleep they're wrecks all day; they can't go in chilly water, they don't feel well when they come out; if they smoke too much they get a headache, if they eat stew they're upset the next day; they catch cold leaving a dance. A temperature of 99° and they're dying. And they never can tell you where it hurts. They go around with pockets full of pills. Which reminds me, I left mine in Paris and I've slept like a log ever since. He got his sunburn the first day. He groaned enough about it; he knows how it feels; he takes care of me, he brings me aspirin, he puts oil on my back and has dinner sent up to the room; he's really very nice. Tomorrow we'll stay in the shade. We'll have a day of rest. You're not supposed to wear yourself out on your vacation, you're supposed to go back to Paris in good shape so that you can have a good winter without any flu or bronchitis. And bring back fond memories, filmed on 8 mm., so that you can show them when you're old.

Everyone thinks I look well. I've lost weight, I can get into my old slacks, I'm apricot color, my hair is almost white; I had it cut short. It's so much more sensible for swimming I told Philippe after I'd done it at the last minute just before leaving just like that, and now it can't grow out by day after tomorrow can it? Besides I snip a little off every day on the sly, looking at myself sympathetically in the mirror. No, it isn't true one should hate oneself; it isn't true. You have to love yourself a little. Right now. As to the hereafter, we'll see. If there is one. In this world, I make little signs of friendship to myself when I meet myself in corridor mirrors. Who's that laughing blond imp over there? It's I, Céline Rodes. And where is Madame Philippe Aignan?

Madame is not in. She went out at five o'clock, to visit Madame Jean-Pierre Bigeon (Julia Morelli). But the telephone there is on the answering service. The Party Does Not Answer they've gone off to town to do errands, no doubt, and they'll come back with a heap of packages. But meantime. Meantime. It's so simple, so simple.

"What's the matter with you these days, Céline?"

"Me? I'm fine."

"You seem nervous and upset. I find you strange."

Something is bothering Philippe. It's obvious that I'm neither nervous nor upset, that's just his way of turning things around. I'm in a good mood. Maybe that's what's bothering him? Not that he suspects anything about Julia, on the contrary he's delighted that I've found a married friend with whom I have something in common, he and Jean-Pierre delight in our charming chitchat, and I must say that with practice we've worked up a convincing girl-talk act, we put on a display of feminine stupidity for them just as they expect, why contradict them when we can't convince them? Two real old farts. We quote from *France-Femme*, beauty care recipes household hints Horoscope. This way they know they have wives. Shitty, but that's how they want it and they're at peace.

No, what's bothering Philippe is something else. I think it's Céline Rodes. He made a big thing about my hair, he says it doesn't grow fast enough, one would think rats were chewing it; he's knocking his head against a wall on that score, a very soft wall, a wall of velvet, I said: Do you think so? it's just the salt water it will get better, what are we doing this evening I'd like to see a Western. You and your Westerns it's a real fixation. Fixation, well that's nice and handy; I may talk about them a lot but we never really go in the end, that's not the way to shut me up about it. Dammit I'll go alone in the afternoon. I don't know why I never thought of it before. What six hundred francs for the movies? said Philippe when he looked at the month's accounts, which I always calculate in old francs which annoys him, I can't get the other ones straight in my head I don't understand them, he's calculating his investment portfolios in millions when they're really hundreds of millions, he got used to it fast because it's practical, but for our little expenses it doesn't make sense—what six hundred francs for the movies, and several times this month, you've been going to the movies? Yes, I go to the movies. What can he say? It isn't for the six hundred old francs no he'd never make a fuss about such a small amount it's not that. Then what can he object to? There's no harm in going to the movies, once the socks are darned. He can't find anything. He's silent. He waited a long time, but at last it came: he found something which I hadn't done; a terrible mess I must admit on the desk where the household papers are, in fact I threw them there because I needed the writing table in the living room, he hadn't been able to lay hands on the Fire Insurance policies, not that we had any fire but he wanted to know what the premiums were and God knows what other vital information. He's cross. "Instead of going to the movies . . . !" Finally it's out. I admit my shortcoming, and I ask if he has noticed any others. He hasn't, at the moment.

"Well then, I think that's very little. I believe I can consider myself almost a perfect wife."

That spiked his guns. Especially the tone. Not a suggestion of nerves. I was making a tapestry; I went on with it. I'm designing it myself; it shows Adam and Eve the Tree the Snake the Apple. Full length. Very pretty. At least it will be pretty if I do it well, which isn't likely. Philippe himself prophesied it; the idea of making a tapestry pleased him very much, but he's very much afraid I won't finish it, like the thousand other things I've started and left unfinished in my life.

"About this failure to organize the papers," I say, "which is the only thing between me and perfection," pause, I take out the brown for the Tree, "I don't think there's any cure for it. I can't help it. The whole thing is too shitty."

"Too what?"

"Shitty."

He is speechless. It's a long time since I've done that to him. These days I express myself discreetly. And even during my revolutionary period I used to give in the second time around.

"I think," I say profiting by his stupor, "that if you want it done the way you think best you'd better do it yourself."

"What? Listen, I have enough on my back already! It seems to me the least you could do is take care of this one small nuisance. Since you have time to go to the movies . . ." (Encore, since I didn't seem to hear it the first time.)

"I have a few nuisances to take care of myself," I say in a calm little voice. "Stewardship is a tissue of nuisances."

"Stewardship?" . . . (He doesn't understand.)

"Housekeeping. It's called stewardship. It's work."

"But for a woman . . . it's only natural . . . to keep house."

"Let it go. But on the other hand, administrative order is man's work. These complicated papers are drafted and drawn up by men. We don't understand anything about them."

"If you were alone you'd damned well have to understand them."

"As far as I remember I never used to. I don't know how I managed without it. Very well, I should think."

His mouth opens. His mouth closes. I know what he wants to say. But he doesn't say it. Thin ice. Meantime I add sweetly:

"And I didn't have you either then darling."

I take out the yellow for the snake. Why am I doing this? A sudden passion. A raging need. To choose wool. Colors, harmonies. The colors of these tapestry yarns are like a stained-glass window. I chose the wools even before I painted the design. And with fantastic care. This one, not that one. And then, to try to do it all myself, someone who'd never made one before, they all told me it was completely mad. Madame Aignan (she too was delighted to see me engaged in a feminine occupation) advised me to buy a prepared canvas, even partly embroidered, for a beginning. She took me to the specialty

shop where they wanted me to choose a rosebush. I asked
for a copy of the Unicorn tapestry. She's crazy, to begin
with that. It would have to be made to order, and at what
a price! And she'll have to wait. I couldn't wait, I had to
do it right away, I was burning to do it. So I made it myself. She's crazy, she doesn't realize. Beginner's enthusiasm
said the shop owner, who was right; leave her alone and
she'll be back after she's spoiled a canvas or two. . . . I
really am a bit scared.

". . . mink."

Philippe is finishing a sentence, or maybe even a perora-
tion, which I had the good fortune of missing because it
must have been extremely nasty.

"What?"

"You even have a mink."

"Yes, nothing for nothing," I answer him serenely, going on with my snake. Not easy. It isn't going to be easy.
Tapestry goes on forever. You need a Crusade to get you
through one. And it isn't really my style after all. But I
have a better idea!

The next day I bought painting materials. That's what
I really wanted to do. I just hadn't realized it. The tapestry was a step in that direction. Didn't I paint once?
Badly but that isn't the point; I painted; had I forgotten?
The ways of Providence are indeed tortuous, I mean, when
one is lost, the road by which one finds oneself is not
straight. Tapestry, that's just a trick. Anything that's feminine but evokes the past will do. A trick.

A whole set of paints, the bill's a big item on the accounts. Much more than wool, and that was expensive
enough. Philippe winces. It's expensive he says.

Mink, one million. Car, two million. Painting, eighteen thousand old francs. That's expensive. How relative everything is.

"And the wools are a loss?" (six thousand.)

I immediately suggest that if that's how things are I can cancel my fall suit which costs three times as much. I'm sick of suits anyway they make me look like an old woman and what's the point of them, either it's warm enough to wear a dress or it's cold enough to wear a coat. I have my mink. If you're broke, I say. Not at all no really we aren't at that point it isn't important never mind since it's done even if the paintings are worthless it's too late let's not talk about it any more. Because he insists I have a suit to wear.

"My wife is doing water colors," he says to our little circle. "It's her new fad."

It's oils of course. But why bother about details, water colors conveys Philippe's meaning better.

"Last month it was tapestry. It didn't last."

The following week I asked for a piano. I thought I might get a laugh out of it. He was looking for an English desk in the Flea Market, so I tried out pianos.

"What are you up to with your pianos Céline?"

"I think we ought to buy a piano."

"A piano, but what for?"

"To decorate the apartment. An apartment isn't complete without a piano. It would look well in the living room. This living room needs a piano."

"If it's just for decoration, you needn't try them out. All you have to do is look at them."

"Oh come on, Philippe, it would be too stupid to buy a piano one couldn't play. That would be money down the drain. It has to be a good one."

"Do you know how much a piano costs? If it's for decoration . . . Really, Céline, you're completely unreasonable. Either it's to play, or it's for decoration. . . ."

"All right, I'll learn. That way it can't be a loss."

"At your age? At your age one's fingers . . . You know, Céline, sometimes I really think you're crazy."

"When I was little I dreamed of learning to play the piano."

"I'd like to know what you didn't dream of when you were little."

"You're absolutely right. I wanted to do everything. Everything interesting, anyway."

"Well, you aren't little any more. You'd better wake up to that fact."

"I just want a piano."

"I really don't know what's the matter with you these days, something is off key in you."

"I don't know when things have gone so well."

"That worries me even more."

"You worry when I feel well? Really?"

"When you are elated this way it isn't a good sign. Are you taking your medicine these days?"

"My sedatives? I threw them out. They upset my liver. I don't take them any more. Have you noticed my color? Don't you think my color is good?"

"Honestly, I don't know what's the matter with you! Anyone would think you wanted to spite me."

"Does it spite you if my color is good?"

"Don't be silly. You threw away your medicine. Your color is good because we just came back from our vacation and you had a good rest. But if you don't take your medicine the way you're supposed to, you'll soon have a relapse."

"Why be so pessimistic, darling? Don't you think there are some people who are just naturally healthy? Don't you believe in such a thing? Really? Anyway, I'm sick of being a drug addict like all these stupid women, we aren't living in America yet. I feel fine and I intend to continue doing so. If it doesn't spite you too much. And I want a piano."

I'm painting Julia. Not naked, because that would attract attention. In a Banlon dress, a lovely green with a round neck, perfectly straight; creaseproof, easy to take off. And to put on. But we aren't often disturbed. There at the back of the apartment the spare room has found its purpose at last, and even a double reason: artist's studio and boudoir, Juana knows that Madame is "working"; she sees the proof of it in the morning and admires it. She only knocks in case of emergency—when Philippe calls, for instance. There's Stephanie, too. She's gotten the habit of dropping in on us. Once, when it was rather a close call, she said, I have a feeling I interrupted you. . . . We must have had an odd look to make Stephanie say that. Nothing to do but get in deeper still: Yes, you interrupted us. You interrupted a conversation we can't continue in front of you.

"Why?"

"You're too young."

"Oh shit, I'm fifteen! What about? At least you can tell me what it was about."

"Love."

"Men," Julia corrects me.

"All the more reason for going on with it. The more I know about these things now, the less mistakes I'll make later on."

"You won't learn anything by it, other people's experience is worthless."

"Better start out with illusions, or you may never start out at all."

"Is it that lousy?"

"No. . . . It has its good sides."

"What? You can tell me."

It interests Stephanie to listen to these two good wives who probably know a lot and who don't shut her up when she asks too much, on the contrary, find it natural and answer her instead of telling her to run along. I know what fifteen-year-old girls are like; I was one. They can take it. Anyway, the only important question about a person of any age is whether she's a fool or not; if not, maturity comes at about age eleven. If she's going to be a fool, it never does. Stephanie likes this viewpoint. This place, which smells of turpentine and also radiates a vibration of life which is perceptible if not definable, attracts her. She settles in, she has no reason to leave and is still too innocent to imagine there could be one, she sits on the floor, I paint, we chat, and now she has begun to draw. Things like that are contagious. A climate. In fact our little world is good for her. Stephanie doesn't bother you too much, I hope? says her mother. No, she doesn't bother us too much, she hasn't that much free time, she has to go to school; she gives us plenty of time to ourselves. There's lots of time, the thing is to know how to use it. Time only asks to be taken; one can have as much as one likes, the more one takes the more one has. All you have to know is how to live. I'm afraid I'm more of an artist at that than at painting. Art may be more difficult, but that's only because when people decide to devote themselves to art they take more pains with it than they do with life.

"Why? That's stupid."

"They don't want to take the time."

"Why?"

"They have other things to do."

"What?"

"Killing time."

These are our little *concetti*. Being Italian, Julia has a knack for them, while I do my best to stick up for the Parisian side. I accomplish least at my painting. It's clever but imitative, you can find a little of everyone in it. I have absolutely no originality when I paint, I love too many painters. I paint like the ones I like minus their genius. Philippe is right about me.

"Too bad there was a Modigliani otherwise you could have had a great career."

Julia does have a long neck.

"He's horrible to you."

"Every time I get interested in something. He gets all worked up. Against it."

"He loves you though. He buys you mink. He pampers you."

"Yes. Even necrophiliacs feel love."

"What?"

"People who go in for corpses. People who can only get their kicks with the dead."

"Do you think maybe you've arrived at the definition of the Husband?"

Jean-Pierre is kinder to me, but then he's not married to me.

"I think it's quite a good likeness. She's caught the expression."

Oh no, not all of it, monsieur, I haven't that kind of talent. And a good thing, or you'd be green around the gills. You'd hardly recognize your wife, monsieur, your half-frigid wife, Monsieur Little-in-Bed-Big-on-the-Road as we call you privately (Philippe is the Dream-Chaser), Monsieur Tarzan of the Clutch, Buffalo Bill of the Iron Horse, Superman of the Carburetor (they had to come back from vacation on the train this time, the car is shot to hell on the Olympus Mountains, that's only the third one he's loused up).

With a woman, fortunately, it's only emotions that are loused up when you handle her badly.

"When you come right down to it," says Julia, "it must be marriage that makes a lesbian of you. I didn't used to be one."

"What makes you think you are one? One little side

dish doesn't classify you for life. It goes on all the time in harems. It's simply a luxury."

"That's what I thought. But I'm beginning to wonder. Yesterday evening on the Champs Elysées I noticed an absolutely divine brunette in a bar. With bangs."

"Yes, I saw her."

"Aha, you saw her. You too."

"So what. She was beautiful. And she was there to be seen. How could you miss her?"

"I even wondered what she'd say . . ."

"If it didn't happen to be her specialty we would have had all the whores around on our backs."

"Maybe even the cops? I'd love it if our Johns had to bail us out at the police station—and hear the charges!"

"And if she took you up on it, how would you enter it in the accounts?"

"Laundry, maybe?"

"Medicine?"

"And how about deductions for Social Security?"

"Beauty treatments."

"Not bad. I'll buy that."

"Anyway, I'm getting completely perverse."

"Prudish France! And I might add Prudish Italy! Oh Ancient Rome, to think we've come to this! To call ourselves perverts over a little affair like this! The Greeks took the whole thing in their stride they went to the slave market and brought home a slave, male or female, just for pleasure and without fuss. Besides all the rest. Luxury, I tell you. Luxury. A lost art. Not everyone could afford it of course there was no justice but today even the capitalists have forgotten how. Even in their expensive pleasures they find ways of screwing themselves up. My dear Julia, your only trouble is that you're normal! It's just that you're silly enough to listen to what people say."

"You're very reassuring."

"And to take it seriously. Psychology. Shit on psychology. We aren't lesbians. We nibble between meals. Period."

"Thank you."

"*Te absolvo.*"

"*Deo gratias.*"

"First of all I'm not attracted to women. Their bodies are too soft. I like when the whiskers scratch. When you feel the bones and it's solid there on top of you. Not to mention the rest, and speaking of that there are certain religions whose disappearance I very much regret—maybe they disappeared because their Object did? I could have become an adept in them."

"I don't care much for women myself. But then what is it that I have with you that men don't have?"

"Leisure."

"Why don't men have leisure?"

"We've already discussed that question."

"But we haven't settled it."

"No."

"Shit."

"Because they work."

"Yes. But why do they work?"

"To earn money."

"What for?"

"To have leisure."

"No good. We're arguing in a circle."

"So that we can have leisure."

"That's it. In fact they're our slaves."

"And they don't know it!"

"What a good joke! Society is really well organized!"

"Not bad. But not true."

"Do you know the story about the Neapolitan? A man from Milan saw him lying in the sun and asked him: Why don't you work, you'd make some money. And then? said the Neapolitan. You'd buy a house. And then? You'd get married, you'd become successful, you'd get rich. And then? And then, said the man from Milan, you could take vacations in the sun. And the Neapolitan said: But I'm already in the sun!"

"Yeah, that's an old story. A nineteenth-century story. Have you been to Naples lately? We passed through this summer; I didn't want to stay. It's overrun with factories. Full of smoke. You can't even see the smoke from Vesuvius any more it's lost in the rest. See Naples and die of asphyxiation. The Neapolitans have finally gotten started and now they're in the grip of Progress poor things. So there's no more sun, with all that smoke. So what's the use and where are they going to sun-bathe? and do you know why? because they lowered the taxes on industries that settle there so they can make a big profit. That's why there's no more sun in Naples and they work instead."

"I think you should repeat that thesis on one of our jolly evenings with the boys, it's the kind of thing that annoys the technocrats, don't forget it. Where were we? Men don't work to have leisure."

"They work for another reason."

"They work in order to work some more."

"So as to make the others sweat by inventing more work for them."

"But why should there be more and more work?"

"So he can sweat himself."

"But why sweat himself?"

"Because they haven't got a better idea."

"I get it: they work because they don't know how to make love."

"And they don't know how to make love because they work!"

"I think we've solved it!"

"But there's no cure."

"If we aren't interrupting your important labors . . ." The two of them dropped in at the house in the middle of the afternoon. They were happy as larks, they made a lot of noise coming in; a little tight, maybe, probably had a drink with the salesman. The New. The Astounding. It has finally arrived. The Victory! That's what they'd come to tell us, and they came at a good moment. They find us behaving like angels, me wielding my brushes, Julia posing while she reads me *La Princesse de Clèves*; it was the first thing she got her hands on. A charming scene, one I ought to have painted as if I were outside it: in the Dutch manner, since I only work in someone else's manner, with the two Johns in one corner of the canvas, high as kites, having just announced to us the arrival of the Jewel of a Jalopy and invited us to come down and admire it "if it wouldn't be too great an interruption of our important labors."

We were in no hurry. But one must be understanding. We put away *La Princesse* and followed them. We looked. It was a car.

"You don't look very enthusiastic."

"It's an automobile," said Julia.

"Don't you think it's a knockout?"

"Once you're inside it you don't see what it looks like."

Jean-Pierre looked at his wife. This is an idea which hadn't occurred to him. I take up her cue.

"Actually it's pure altruism to buy a new car; other people get all the pleasure from it."

"But we're people too!" cried Jean-Pierre ingeniously, and then he embarked on a Catalogue of Virtues, and we began to regret leaving *La Princesse de Clèves*. If you're going to trade one tedium for another, it at least has a beautiful style.

"We're leaving Saturday. We'll all go would you like that?"

"Go where?" ask the women.

"We'll make it a race," say the men.

"Let's go to the seashore," say the women.

"I'll come in first, you'll see," says Philippe.

"Let's go to a place with cliffs," say the women.

"Ha!" says Jean-Pierre, "220! You can't make that in yours—it's sending a boy to do a man's job."

"We'll go crabbing."

"Boy my ass," says Philippe, lapsing into the vernacular in his wrath, "and anyway, in a race it isn't just speed, it's skill that counts."

"Shall we take bathing suits? The water should still be warm enough."

"Well, I'm not worried. And with this overdrive, the pickup, its . . ."

"We can paddle in the water even if we can't actually swim."

"You seem to forget you'll be breaking it in."

"Have you a net?"

"We can buy one there."

"My mechanic you know the one I told you about he's a great guy he's already begun it for me I hate breaking in cars it makes me nervous, and with two hours a day on the turnpike from now until Saturday . . ."

"We can fish for shrimp."

"I already can get it up to . . ."

". . . if we get some low tides . . ."

"They ought to be high now, anyway, it's just past the equinox."

"Well, if you can do it I can. You watch, I'll be there first."

"We don't have to race," the women try to say. "All we have to do is leave a little earlier. It isn't far to the seashore."

Once more we must all be well prepared in advance. No stopping to take a leak. But anyway, the sea will be there at the end, and the sea is the sea, nobody can spoil that. We left at dawn on Saturday, September 30. It was a beautiful day.

"We've got lots of time, we left very early—oh, did you see that? Apples! Maybe they're ripe—say, there seems to be some building going on down there—do you remember where the turnoff is or do you want me to look at the map?"

I try to be calm, even playful. I'm scared silly. I definitely am becoming more and more frightened of driving with Philippe. Not to mention in this damned race between these two fools today. Horrible.

"Oh. A cat. Squashed flat. They got him, the bastards. Quickly, I hope."

I've counted four of them since we left.

"Please God one doesn't decide to cross in front of us . . ."

I pray: Don't cross. Don't cross, we're coming. At this speed he couldn't stop if he tried. But he wouldn't care. Please don't cross.

"Another cat."

"If you're saying that to slow me down you're wasting your breath. I can see as much as you can."

"Then I hope I can see everything."

"There's no use carrying on that way."

"Obviously there's no use in anything. Except maybe praying."

He shakes his head as if I were a fly. Since our vacation, I nag him whenever he goes over 130 and he's going to get it now. I'm scared, I'm scared and I'm scared.

"Look, there's an accident. Over there to the left, did you see?"

At 140 you can't see anything but a heap of metal with some people around it. We're already way past it. Fortunately this isn't a very attractive road with all the beet fields beside it, there isn't anything to miss.

At the boardwalk at Deauville, the meeting place, Philippe looks at his watch proudly. We're first.

Then we wait.

He had a hard time finding them. Jean-Pierre was at Bichat Hospital with six broken ribs and a hole in his lung.

"And Julia?"

"She's dead."

Jean-Pierre Bigeon, thirty-four years old, eleven accidents, two causing injury and one death: his wife's. The Victory, passing on a curve—I saw that curve, you can't see around the corner there; that was the accident we saw this morning by the side of the road, the heap of metal and the people, we recognized the car when we were on our way back to Paris, going slowly slowly this time, looking for them, with death in our hearts—the Victory crashed head on into a 2CV coming from the other direction. The speedometer was jammed at 160. There were four serious injuries in the 2CV, among them a little girl with a broken back. Congratulations.

"Why couldn't he have died too?"

"Oh now see here darling! How would that have helped?"

"It would have helped that he would never get into another car, which would have made life that much safer for other people!"

"Jean-Pierre is no worse than anyone else."

"That's what makes it so awful. There are a lot like him!"

"There are more than 175,000 accidents a year in France Céline, and that makes more than 230,000 injured and dead. You can't suppose it only happens to strangers? Of course you feel much worse when the people hurt are your friends."

Of course. With as many as that you can't hope to pass a whole lifetime without some friends being included. It's statistics. All you can say is okay.

"And out of that 175,000 accidents I wonder how many are caused by neurotics or half-wits? I'd like to know. If we're talking statistics that would really be an impressive one!"

I went to the hospital. I waited until he was a little better: fully conscious. Until no one was there. I didn't say Hello or How are you; I said to him, "You killed your wife." He burst into easy tears. I know it's awful. I won't ever be able to forgive myself you don't need to tell me Céline I think of it day and night without stopping I can't bear it, etc., just words. They do things and afterwards "they can't stand it." Easy.

"Not to mention the little girl, though we don't know her. She's paralyzed from the waist down."

He hadn't known she'd always remain paralyzed. They hadn't told him yet. So as not to upset him. How considerate. I gave him the details. I had brought the newspaper. More tears.

"You were passing on a curve. Your speedometer

showed a hundred and sixty. I saw that curve: visibility zero. Didn't you ever learn the Rules of the road?"

He stammered, there was no time to think of rules at such a moment when his whole life, when he really had room, when the 2CV was "not really" on his right, and the speedometer was certainly inaccurate because of the crash. No time for rules, but "at such a moment" they can still find explanations for the insurance company, including lies. And they are always ready with the accusation: It was the Other Fellow.

"You had time to notice all that and none to have a reflexive response? My compliments."

Why have I come if it is only to tell him such horrible things, hasn't he already been punished enough, must even his friends—

"What kind of car was in front of you?"

"A Maserati."

"You wanted to pass it and you couldn't. That bothered you, didn't it? But a Monsieur Jean-Pierre Bigeon can't pass a Maserati. A Jean-Pierre Bigeon stays behind Maseratis. For keeps."

Oh, why won't I be still? I beg of you, leave me alone to suffer!—but what could he do, he couldn't move from the bed, he was swathed in bandages, molded in plaster, he had to listen to me. It was fate! he cried.

"Not fate, stupidity. You killed your wife because you're an ass. You don't know how to drive. If you can't be a man you should ride a bicycle. Your reflexes are too slow. You aren't strong enough to handle the wheel. You're a little nobody with a power complex, like a lot of other bastards."

"You hate me. I understand. You're hurt. But—Céline —why—blame me—when I am already—maybe I'm dying—"

"Forget the psychology and stick to technique. Never touch another car; you can't handle them." On that I left.

"I just saw Jean-Pierre," says Philippe. "He had such a violent fit of depression yesterday that he threw himself out of bed."

If he wants me to cry he'll have to stick his finger in my eye. Let Jean-Pierre Bigeon throw himself in hell if he likes.

"It was after your visit. Which you didn't tell me about. Which proves you weren't very proud of it. Céline, what made you do that?"

"A whim."

"Don't be difficult, Céline. I understand your distress. I understand it. But you won't find any comfort in cruelty."

"Oh? What shall I find it in? Resignation?"

"That might be better. I know it isn't easy, but . . ."

"It's all very well when it's God who does the taking away, or so you tell me, but when it's Jean-Pierre Bigeon . . ."

"That's still not a reason to be cruel. Revenge . . ."

"I wasn't cruel. You're just talking psychology. To hell with psychology."

"What? Not cruel? You went and told him that he'd killed his wife and paralyzed a little girl . . ."

"All right, it's true."

"Just when they were doing everything to hide the truth from him!"

"Why?"

"Haven't you any heart?" He sits down. "Why? Out of pity, if I have to spell it out for you. Aren't you capable of feeling pity?"

"He's a bastard."

"Yes, I know, and you told him so. But is that a reason?"

"I'm not Jesus Christ, who has pity even on bastards. Nor you either. You don't feel pity, you feel what you think is expected of you—and male solidarity. At least I have some pity for the people who weren't responsible. I have pity for Julia, and the poor souls in the 2CV, and the ones left behind."

"And having pity on them means taking revenge for them?"

"It's not revenge at all. Listen Philippe, I wasn't looking for revenge, nor consolation, nor for anything personal if you can understand that. I simply went to explain to Jean-Pierre Bigeon that he ought never to touch another car because he doesn't know how to handle them. That's all."

"And couldn't that have waited? Are you a monster? Don't you know you can't say things like that to a man in his condition? He's not going to drive a car tomorrow! You could have waited until he was able to stand it!"

"Don't you know what being able to stand it means to bastards like him? It means being able to forget it. A bastard like that is dense. With such bastards you have to hit them when they're weak. A bastard only understands what you burn into his flesh. That's just why I had to take advantage of his condition so as to make an impression, it was that moment or never, and I seized it."

"Well, I hope you're satisfied. His condition is much worse since your visit. You must have made an impression."

"I hope so."

"If he dies you'll be a criminal! Do you understand? Criminal!"

"If he dies, he'll die of broken ribs, not falling out of bed. Nobody dies of falling out of bed."

"You are completely amoral, my girl. I'd prefer to think you're hysterical with grief. I must say I didn't realize you cared so much for Julia. Nor that you were capable of such strong emotions. You never gave me that impression before. I only hope you'd feel as much for me."

"It isn't grief, it's rage. I'd feel it for anyone."

"Charming."

"Look, Philippe, make up your mind."

"What?"

"Either say my emotions are too strong or that they aren't strong enough but not both at the same time— oh for God's sake I'm sick of this stupid discussion. I did what I thought I had to do and if it was wrong I'll hear about it at the Last Judgment it isn't up to you to decide."

"Have I heard you right?"

"You heard me."

"Madame hands down judgments, but the rest of us must be quiet . . . !"

"Please, Philippe, don't confuse little personal gripes with serious matters. It's a bore."

"What did you say?"

"I said shit."

Philippe slammed the door on the way out. Jean-Pierre Bigeon didn't die, he'd never had any intention of it. Animals like him have thick skins. And he drove other cars, and may have killed other people, I don't know I never saw him again. Philippe spared me that, in order to spare him. Jean-Pierre came out of the whole affair very well, his company succeeded in proving that the 2CV wasn't absolutely on the right. The little girl got a modest settlement. Julia was dead. And a good thing, because her face was ground to pulp when they pulled her out of the wreckage of the Victory. I prayed she died right away, like the cat.

Pₐᵢₙₜₑᵣₛ wₒₜₕ ₙₒ ₜₐₗₑₙₜ shouldn't paint portraits. The subject may die. Then only the portrait is left, and it's no good. I'm ashamed.

I tried painting others from memory. I worked hard at it.

"Honestly, I had no idea you cared so much for Julia," Philippe says again, seized with posthumous jealousy—he didn't know I was trying to do it over because the portrait was no good and that I was ashamed of it; I myself don't know if I loved Julia or how much, I only know I couldn't stand I couldn't stand, that someone, who was alive, now is dead; nor can I stand the picture I keep seeing of the moment, the second when she saw the car coming at her, because she saw it; nor that her face was destroyed even before the worms got to it. I couldn't stand the thought of these three things that's all. If that's loving, I don't know. They're just things.

Now I was the keeper of that face, and I couldn't

paint it. I succeeded a little better with the *Princesse de Clèves* scene as I imagined it that day, and which I tried to reconstruct with Stephanie's help; Stephanie hardly left me during this period; I don't know what I would have done without her. She played hooky from school. I got her to pose for the two silhouettes, sometimes as me painting, and sometimes as the other who is gone forever. When she "was" Julia, she cried. She found it hard to bear, but she didn't want to give up, nor give in to the pressure from her mother, who didn't like "this morbid business" at all, and continually forbade her to "bother" me.

My painting began to distress me. It was taking too long. I knew it wasn't any good. I didn't need to be told.

"My wife paints, too," said Philippe, after a dinner party when the conversation turned to art. On certain occasions, in front of certain people, he liked to call attention to this picturesque aspect of our household. This time he was talking to a gentleman whom we hadn't entertained before, and who had used his huge profits from real estate deals to form a collection. An enlightened connoisseur as they say. And as a result, people are always after him and I found Philippe tactless. His remark produced the expected effect: Monsieur politely refrained from making a grimace, producing instead a worldly smile which fooled no one.

"I don't paint, I dabble. It's just a hobby, I'm not an artist."

I thought I'd get him off the hook and change the subject. But Philippe God knows why persisted. No, she's being modest; she really paints—and all at once he got up. "I want to show you so you can tell me—"

"Philippe, no, please . . ."

I couldn't stop him. I would have had to get up too, to make a spectacle of myself as a wife who runs after her husband making scenes. The calm bearing I tried to achieve slowed me down to the point where I only met Philippe on his way back, near the door of the living room, he shot off so fast that he was back again. He held the first portrait and the last, neither one any good; luckily the *Princesse de Clèves* wasn't dry yet.

"Philippe, I don't want you to. They aren't good enough. . . . Please . . ."

I had to speak softly because the living room is so near the people could have heard us.

"Who knows?" said Philippe, pushing me aside.

"No!" I tried to take the canvases.

"Look," said Philippe, showing me the door, which was open, so that I could understand how unseemly a scene would be. He grabbed the pictures out of my hand brutally, and I saw violent determination in his eyes, concealed by an ambiguous smile. The expression surprised me, and indicated that a struggle would be useless; he had decided. He went into the living room with me behind him, looking foolish. With a winning, "Not bad?" he stuck the portrait under the gentleman's nose. Monsieur looked at it a moment and then turned towards the company, saying:

"By the way, did you see the Valadon show? What made me think of it," he said, coming back to my poor creation, "is that she is one of the only women painters who ever had any talent. Charming," he added looking in my direction long enough for Philippe to take the thing out of his sight. In spite of this absence of encouragement, the second was put in its place. Very nice, the amateur said, looking at it for a short enough time so that even Philippe saw enough is enough. I was burning with shame, paralyzed, but prevented by all those people from making the slightest gesture to indicate how I felt. Then I saw Stephanie coming across the room, throwing herself at Philippe to snatch the two portraits from him, and hugging them to herself so that the painting was hidden. "Come on," she said to me authoritatively. I obeyed. We left the room without a word from anyone.

In the studio, I broke down. I never had looked for such humiliation, it was thrown in my face, and I found it hard to bear. I knew my canvases were bad. I didn't need to be told about it by such an authority and with all those people around.

"What a bastard that man is!" said Stephanie.

"Which one?"

"The collector."

"Oh, he's understandable. Women throw themselves at him wherever he goes, he's sick of it, he defends himself. Only I didn't ask for it! I know perfectly well that what I do is worthless! I don't need to have an expert's certificate!"

"Céline? . . . Don't look that way! . . . Come on, we'll go out. We'll take a walk."

"But they . . ."

"They can go to hell, if you want to know what I think. They're dirty bastards. You don't have to go back to them after what they've done to you. Besides honor wouldn't permit you to, if you want an official reason. If my brother had been there he would have fixed them— that fool, he's always running off, and I can't blame him if he can get away with skipping this crap—but he would have thought of some great idea for screwing them. Come on. Put on a coat, it's cold. Put on your mink, we'll do a little streetwalking, we'll earn some money and we won't need them any more."

"And I'll go to prison for impairing the morals of a minor."

"I'll say I'm the one who impaired yours."

"That doesn't count."

"I'll bring you a cake. With a file in it."

"I'll get my fingers sticky."

"You can wash them."

"There's no water."

"You can suck them. Come on, let's go drink some Coca-Cola. You can drink whisky, you'll get drunk and forget your address and then you won't be able to go home again. Because just between you and me, Philippe is really a heel. Really a heel. Come on, let's get out without making any noise. We'll ditch them.

"And it was Julia's portrait," she says. "He did it to Julia's portrait! He made no mistake about that."

"Two birds with one stone. Philippe doesn't kid around."

"A heel."

"Why did I do such a bad portrait? Why haven't I more talent?"

"Maybe it will come?"

"I'm not going to paint any more."

"That miserable bastard! Maybe you'll do something else? Maybe you'll become a good pianist?"

"Too old, nothing to be done about it; my fingers. I don't know what I could be! I wanted everything and I'm nothing! I don't know what I am! I don't know what to do with myself! Maybe I have a gift for one thing: life. But it's a losing game. It isn't a commodity that's quoted on the market. Nobody wants it. I don't know what to do with myself!"

"You talk like a drunken Russian out of Dostoievsky."

"You've read him?"

"I've seen them in the movies. If you're going to talk like a drunk, you'd better wet your whistle."

"Where have you been?"

"Taking a walk."

"What happened to you?"

"You can ask me that?"

"You can't be making such a fuss just because they weren't impressed with your paintings!"

"You're incredible! Analysis: 'Such a fuss'—first, I simply went for a walk; second, you're the one making the fuss I haven't opened my mouth. 'They'—who is they? Everyone, according to you. 'Impressed'—"

"What's the matter with you, Céline? My word, have you been drinking? You can hardly stand up and I can smell the alcohol from here!"

"'Impressed': a word calculated to make it look as if 'impressing' people was the only reason for my painting. Finally, the whole sentence . . ."

"I'm letting you talk just to see how far you'll go. . . ."

". . . from beginning to end: the whole sentence suggests that I was only looking for praise and that I was disappointed not to have received it. Whereas . . ."

"What is this nonsense?"

"The nonsense is yours, I'm trying to make sense of it."

"Please Céline I don't need you to explain what I'm saying."

"Oh sure you know exactly what you're saying: nothing is left to chance, I only want to show you that I know too. Whereas . . ."

"What have you done with Stephanie?"

"She went home."

"She's going to catch it."

"She expects that."

"You don't mean to tell me you've involved that child in your, in your—"

"Turpitude depravity vileness debauchery ignominy. Bacchanale? Dissoluteness, sinfulness . . . Sinfulness, maybe?"

"That's enough."

"Have you got one?"

"That's enough Céline!"

"What's enough? He doesn't know. That's enough Céline, yes. He's enough for Céline. Enough. She's the one who saved me that child, God bless her. Saved me from you. So have some respect for her, she has more intelligence than a whole cartload of Aignans. Of Onions. Ha!"

"You're drunk so I won't hold it against you."

"That's right don't hold it let it fall it'll do just as well on the floor. Besides I haven't finished my grammatical analysis. Excuse me, semantic. Tends to show that I was looking for praise for myself."

"You already said that."

"Don't interrupt. . . . It was you, against my will, with a suspicious insistence, what am I saying suspicious clear as a mountain stream, a murderous insistence, who were going to expose the evidence of my misery to that cement merchant in order to have an expert since you had one around deal me a mortal blow, you prick. You see what you are . . . Philippe Aignan! You slapped me!"

"It's the only thing to do with a drunken woman."

"But Philippe Aignan, you slapped me, didn't you notice?"

"Listen Céline . . ."

"I didn't feel it because I'm drunk, but I noticed it! You slapped me Philippe Aignan! It's the first time."

"Listen, Céline, you treated me like scum."

"And I warn you, it's the last. I think I'll leave. Right now."

"Right now would surprise me. You wouldn't get far. Listen, Céline, stay here, please. Go to bed, we'll see about it tomorrow."

"I don't know whether we'll see tomorrow. Tomorrow we may be blind."

"Go to bed. You couldn't walk if you tried."

"I don't want to sleep here. Isn't there another bed in the house? This one is too small and it's going round."

"No it isn't going round. Lie down now. I know it wasn't nice of me to slap you. It was just a reflex!"

"A bad reflex!"

"True. Get into bed. Remember, I've been crazy with anxiety . . . calling police stations . . . while you were . . ."

"While I was a bad painter!"

"No no!"

"Listen to me carefully: I am a bad painter and I know it. Getting an expert in to demonstrate this to me officially,"

"If you already know it, why should it bother you if somebody else says it? I don't understand you."

"comma, is a gratuitous act of perverse malice committed with the deliberate intention of hurting. You don't understand me tralala. But me, I understand you, you're a prick Philippe."

"Oh now listen don't start that again!"

"Or a moron. But I don't think so. And besides, you slap. In short, you're a husband!"

"Céline, lie down. Tomorrow we'll talk about this calmly."

"No we will not talk about it tomorrow. Tomorrow I'll be sleeping. Because I'm tired. Tired tired tired tired. And I'm fed up, fed up, fed up, fed up, fed up. I'm leaving."

"Be quiet now."

"I'm nauseated."

"I know."

"Haha. It's not true. But I'm fed up, that's true. I'm not going to paint any more. Never, I swear it darling aren't you happy? I won't paint any more. I'll play the piano."

"That's it. Tomorrow you can go pick one out. Go to sleep."

That's how I got my piano.

A piano for a slap, I didn't shop for a bargain. I have my pride. Philippe too; he signed the check. God knows whether he would have if he'd thought I'd forgotten his promise, made to a drunk, and given in the expectation of a total amnesia. The welcher. That's what comes of underestimating one's equal and counting too much on her downfall. A half million. But that just happened to be the one I liked best, that's all; and Stephanie, who had also received her slap that evening, received no piano so, according to my ideas, had her share in this one.

"It was worth it though," she said, "just to have helped you get it."

That's what she said to her mother, too, after the slap: That's nothing, it was worth it, I forgive you; a remark which earned her another one, after which she went on to say it was even worth two. Her mother didn't push the price any higher, she hadn't given a slap in five years. But you have to put yourself in the place of a Mother who sees her daughter come in at two o'clock in the morning while the Father frantic is calling all the hospitals in the city. Stephanie understood this and held no grudge.

"When you're married you'll get better wages."

"Don't tell me that after the examples I have around me, one who kills his wife and another who slaps his, not to mention my parents who never speak to each other, if that's supposed to encourage me. I'd rather be a prostitute. Bruno tells me they make a good daily wage."

I thought I'd better tell her about the inconveniences of the profession which Bruno had neglected to explain and with which I had a secondhand acquaintance. She was too idealistic, that kid. I talked about the fatigue of being on one's feet, the high heels, the bad weather; the necessity of having a pimp bothered her. Before getting into venereal disease and other details inappropriate to her age, I point out several gentlemen passing in the street and ask her: "How about that one?" At the thirtieth, she backed down. I'm afraid I deprived the Rue Blondel of a remarkable prospect. But I think I did Stephanie a valuable service: the important thing is to be thoroughly informed, now she can do as she likes. I finally conclude, after taking into account the inconveniences, which are about equal to those of piecework under contract, that of all the forms of prostitution, the least exhausting, if one enters into it in the right spirit, that is to say a strictly practical one, is still mar—

Who is this talking? Who is saying such things? Who is this cynical, blasé person?

"What happened to you? Did the cat get your tongue?"

"It can't be I saying those things."

"Who is, then?"

"I don't know. I never had such ideas. Never."

"What are your ideas?"

"That you have to be inspired to make love. That you have to look for the little light, which—wait till I remember, it's so dim, let's see, little light little light, surely it will come back to me. Men are fragments—ah yes:

'Perfection is in heaven and on earth there are only little scattered lights and these are man's love but that after all is the most marvelous thing in the world above all if at the same time the weather is fine and if the wind is good and one should make love with the moon as a substitute light,' amen. That's me. Oh yes, I recognize myself all right: what a sap!"

"And how are you supposed to eat?"

"You get along. Like the little birds. You turn it over to God."

"Who doesn't exist, if I understand you?"

"Who doesn't exist."

"Convenient."

"Not at all, but interesting. Furnishes a good deal of joy, even if it is founded on illusion. Long live illusion if it makes one enj—if it—never mind. Oh I know who was speaking instead of myself just now. A disease I caught recently. A fatal disease. If it isn't treated in time."

"What is it?"

"Experience."

"I love you."

"Never catch that disease!"

"I love you. I've loved you for a long time."

"Look what it's made of me: a cynical tart who buys pianos!"

"I know you heard me."

"Of course, I'm not deaf. So I have a mink; a piano; dresses; at Christmas I'll get pearls—it was Julia who wanted me to have pearls, and I'll get them! I'll accept them as a present from her. From beyond. Her hand extended to me from Beyond, holding pearls. They'll have to be real, coming from there."

"You loved Julia."

"I don't know. What does it mean, to love? Do you know?"

"Céline, you don't want to answer me!"

"Answer what? You haven't asked me anything. I haven't heard any question. Have you asked me a question?"

"I made a declaration to you."

"I made a note of it. What does one do with a declaration?"

"How hard you are!"

"Right here, out of the blue, right in the middle of Paris. On the Place du Trocadéro. What a place. Well, let's go somewhere else, let's go to the Latin Quarter, I haven't been there in a hell of a long time. I'm sick of it here."

"All right don't answer me I don't care I love you just the same whether you want me to or not. It's my business after all!"

"All right, I give up. You made it. I congratulate you, it wasn't easy. And I thank you, because one should give thanks for such a declaration, it is an honor to be loved. For God my dear Phaidros is in the lover, not in the beloved; though the lover sees him there, or thinks he does. But is he right after all? For my dear Phaidros the God is in the beloved where the lover may see Him embodied in flesh, without which he could never have known Him directly—thus passion is the way to Knowledge and gives us access to a place we never could have reached without its help."

"Is that you talking?"

"It's Plato, as edited by Rodes, 1962, Paris. Kali-Yuga. And that my dear Phaidros is why it is good either to love or to be loved, but not both at the same time, if possible. If possible. If possible. That is catastrophe, because two mirrors placed face to face will shatter against each other in their effort to be joined. Not to mention fourteen years of misery. See if you can catch that cab."

"Then I'm the lover?"

"So you said."

"And you are the beloved?"

"It's a grammatical imperative, and a good one too, you'll find."

"If I understand you, my dear Plato, you accept being the beloved?"

"What can I do about it? It's a grammatical imperative. And, Stephanie, terribly dangerous."

"For whom?"

"For the weak."

"I am strong!"

"Nobody is strong. Nobody. That's why—"

"My dear Phaidros."

"My dear Stephanie, let's be quiet. Enough nonsense. Come on, I'll buy you the book I've been quoting to you because I don't remember a single word of it."

A bookshop. Full of books. How many centuries is it since I set foot in a bookshop? Oh, there was a time when

I snitched books, a frantic need, a love; and since I can afford them I don't go into bookshops any more! How monstrous! What disgusting ingratitude! Oh but I'll make up for it! I'll make up for it a hundredfold! Stephanie had to come up to the apartment to help me carry them.

"What's all that? Are you going back to school?"

Of course that's Philippe speaking you must have recognized him. Philippe who came home before me for once because we stopped for a drink at the Flore and another at the Nuage and then we met Kiki and to make a long story short, here we are.

"Your mother called, Stefi. She's wondering what happened to you. Or rather she isn't wondering."

"Then everything is fine," I say.

"No that's just it everything isn't just fine! Mother thinks Stephanie has better things to do than—what have you been up to anyway?"

"We bought some books."

"I can see that."

"Then why do you ask?"

"You . . . you . . . Stephanie, call your mother. Yes, right now. Because I say so. You" (to me) "promised me."

"What?"

"Not to drink any more!"

"I? When did I promise that?"

"When you were drunk."

"Then what do you expect, I wasn't responsible, Philippe."

"Yes Mama . . . No Mama . . . Listen Mama . . ."

"Anyway I didn't drink."

"You smell of it."

"I smell because you haven't had a drink yet. It's simply a time warp. I'm in the fourth dimension and you're still in the third."

"Oh, you and your sophisms!"

"But really, Philippe, what do you call drinking?"

"Drinking. Drinking, for heaven's sake!"

"I didn't buy enough books. I didn't find the dictionary which would make us understand each other, you and I. But I'm afraid it hasn't been written yet. I'm going to write one myself. I'll start tomorrow. I'll buy some paper . . ."

"—No, Mama—Listen, Mama—But Mama Now really Mama oh, for God's sake!—Good—Yes—Good—Okay. Oh my goodness, how nervous mothers get!"

"Do me a favor and leave now. I'm sick of having you around here all the time."

"So is Mama. It seems I bore Céline."

"Me? How does she know that? It seems to me I'd be the first to know."

"That's right, encourage her. How do you think she's ever going to finish school fooling around like this?"

"That's not for two years, she can fool around a little longer."

"But I learn things when I'm with Céline! She quotes philosophers all the time!"

"Philosophers. This I'd like to hear."

"Well I've tried to talk to you about it Philippe, but you always cut me short. And now you want to hear, do you? Well, you won't. I'm sulking. Because you see my dear Pécuchet that if two mirrors placed face to face break against each other, what is left of the beautiful image once reflected in them—what am I saying? What am I telling you? What can two mirrors reflect when they're placed face to face? What can they reflect, my dear Phaidros? I must be crazy. I had it wrong from the beginning."

"I don't doubt it. You still here? Didn't I tell you to leave a good quarter hour ago? Good night!"

"Stephanie! You forgot your book. There's one for you in this pile—where is it? Wait. I have it."

"If they try to keep us apart," she says to me at the door, "this story will become Romeo and Juliet!"

"Please be strong. It started beautifully. We'll just go underground."

"You'll meet me at the door after school."

"With candy. And a white beard. I'll end up taking hemlock, my own Xantippe will give it to me in small daily doses . . ."

"Haven't you left yet, Stephanie?"

"Go. It is the lark. See you tomorrow."

Philippe came in at two in the morning yesterday. And without phoning. He was at a business dinner, no women invited, anyway that's what he told me and I have every reason to believe him. (Yes yes I know, you're laughing at me, but that attractive version of husbands on a spree dates from the days of vaudeville while in today's Paris monogamy is the style. And if I am wrong, what's the difference, that has no place in this story.) So he comes in, smiling, agreeable, and finds me in bed reading. I took advantage; when he's home closing time is earlier.

"Aren't you asleep darling?"

"No, you see I'm not."

"Were you waiting for me?"

"No, I was reading."

Pause. Nothing. He moves around the room. Is about to undress. Comes back. Dawdles.

"You look very peaceful."

"I love to read in bed."

"When I'm not here you're perfectly happy."

". . ." (No comment: what comment is there?)

"You weren't worried?"

"If I was darling it's all over now that you're here."

"You could at least say you were worried."

"You would have said I was making a scene and curtailing your liberty. You would have put me in my place."

"Maybe. But it would have showed me you cared. Sometimes I need to know that. One can have doubts. When you see a woman living beside you, sitting, or walking around the house without seeming to notice your presence . . . who always seems so busy . . ."

"Mostly busy with the house."

"And with other things too, other things . . ."

"Is that bad?"

"Who never makes the first move."

"At least I don't slap anybody."

"That again? You really hold a grudge!"

"Oh no. It's not that. You mentioned gestures and that made me think of it."

"Maybe it would be better if you did slap me! If you'd

curtail my liberty, as you say! If you'd make scenes, even jealous ones! Better that than nothing! Madame goes out, takes walks, eats ice cream with a kid as if she were one herself! At thirty-one!" (He's not giving me the benefit of any doubts—always the gentleman.) "Or else she's deep in her books. All this nonsense!"—This last crack is punctuated by his snatching the particular nonsense I had in my hands and throwing it across the room.

So. Now I suddenly understand why the piano was accepted so quietly. It's because he saw immediately that there was no future in that late-blooming enterprise.

"And what is that one?" At a distance and from upside down he tries to figure out the title of the enemy on the floor. "*Ten Ways of Keeping Cows*. Are you thinking of going in for agriculture?"

"Yes. I have a craving for the country these days."

God knows I'd never thought of it but he just gave me the idea.

"Fresh air. The air here is giving me dreadful anemia, I think that the Rue de la Pompe is particularly unhealthy, anyway, I have an appointment with the doctor tomorrow"—I'm improvising brilliantly—"if he finds I'm as badly off as I think, I'm considering a trip to Italy to see Julia's family. You remember they invited me the day—when they came. I'd only need to wire them."

"Julia. And you don't ask if that would be convenient for me, if I've made other plans which might require your presence . . . !"

"If the doctor orders me to the country I'll bring you a medical certificate. In cases like that, even employers agree."

He's dying I've killed him he's going to die. I try not to laugh. Poor man. I ignored his big entrance, his violence hurt nothing but the poor book, and his heavy sarcasm about the cows snapped back in his face, when I agreed with such docility, only in order to plunge him into a depth of ridicule that he'll measure when, my back turned, he'll come to snoop in my book (and will then realize how ignorant he is and how far I am from him for it's a Buddhist text)—oh, the poor fellow! He doesn't know I've begun to use Judo. One of the most useful accomplishments in married life.

He looks as if he's been sucking a lemon. He's the one will be sick tomorrow, who will be in bed with me taking care of him, my medical certificate in my pocket though because I'm not kidding.

And the week after, I'm off.

"You're leaving me," says Stephanie. "You won't be here any more. I won't see you any more."

"That's exactly right."

We are sucking candy, sitting on a bench in the square. I met her at the door of her school and brought it to her. As promised. It's much funnier when it's true.

"And I'll miss you."

"Look, Stephanie, I'll exist just the same if I'm in Rome. Will a simple matter of geography be enough to change your state?"

"No. But it will make it worse."

"Aggravate it. Good, it will change its form, it will be Absence."

"That seems awfully intellectualized . . ."

"Yes, but maybe that's better. Because I don't agree with our good Master that we're made up of a soul and a body."

"Lord, with me it's a hell of a mixture between the two of them. If you knew!"

"Be quiet. We'll never know, I'm leaving, it's a good thing."

"No! It is the nightingale and not the lark!"

"Stephanie, that's the blackbird you hear. Good-by."

"Good-by, Céline. Let me think of you."

You're unconscious. You don't realize anything. You know nothing about yourself. I left, quite serenely. Wisely. Chastely.

I didn't miss Philippe. His absence went unnoticed, so to speak. From the beginning. And people talk about the force of habit. Nothing is more fragile, easier to break. The second evening finding myself sprawled out in bed, I realized I was sleeping alone. The night before I hadn't thought of it. From my calm I realized how detached I was from sexual matters; this gave me more solace than regret.

I went about the big house tranquilly, I walked in the garden, in the hills, under the olive trees. I daydreamed about Stephanie; about love, I mean real love; I mean the kind which consists of loving, not of wanting to be loved, two distinct states between which lies the frightful familiar mixture of both. It seemed to me that I had given Stephanie a unique opportunity, to love in the active form, without interference from the unhealthy passive one. I asked myself which was best, to love or to be loved. I decided that it was the former.

It seemed to me that I had never loved in that way myself; no one had ever forced me to it. Which meant finally that I had never loved at all. Loved someone. Without asking for any return—how marvelous! I envied Stephanie. I put myself in her place. I reveled in it. I had to be careful not to love her in return because of the charm of her state. That would have spoiled everything. I had to stay in my humble role of object of love.

I thought all kinds of crazy things. The country seemed to demand it. It is so gentle, almost divine. The pines are eternally green here, the olives eternally silver, the sky eternally blue, and the sun is always shining. It's good here. Why does anyone live anywhere else my God! How can they stand all those horrible climates? Why do they all huddle together like sheep in the freakish, foggy, rainy, shitty north? It's true that it's the people who make it shitty there, not the country. So long as they're there it's still possible to go to nice places and where they are not.

In the evening there is a wild moon. I was lucky enough to arrive when it was new. I saw the Crescent. Each evening I watch it grow. There's a thing worth doing. Naked in the sky, shining. Or else through the leaves of the olive trees. Or at the top of a pine. I can put it where I like, make it move, place it. I love it. Opposite the house, at the top of a hill, there is a perfect row of pines. Pines: extraordinary. The moon: extraordinary. What luck to have a moon! We don't really realize it but it's a great stroke of luck! We could just as well not have had one. What a jewel, this planet: the colors, the forms, everything. Lord, it's a great success, there's only one thing You botched, really—the last. Were You tired? For all the rest, there's nothing to add. Especially the moon; it's a real gift. Thank You. There are people who think it's silly to look at the moon: let them go screw themselves in a coal cellar.

Then there are people who just don't see it. And maybe there are people who see something altogether different from what I see. A plate. Philippe must see a plate. And the leaves of the olive trees which it silvers, the little pieces of brightness which move. I love it. I love. I love. The sky at night, it drives me mad. I run around the hills like a madwoman. And in the daytime, it's the sun that sets me off. The sun is extraordinary too. Just because I speak well of the moon doesn't mean I don't like the sun. Just don't ask me to choose. But no one asks me. I've been given both of them. Isn't that perfect?

I am doing absolutely nothing except existing. This takes up all my time. I live in the midst of people who are simply nice. Nice. Should that be surprising? I'm amazed by it every hour of the day: I wasn't used to it any more; where I live it doesn't exist any more, it's simply forgotten, lost; there, there's only pretension, fatuousness, arrogance, irony, phony intellectualism, everything is superficial, people quarrel over nothing, are surly, sharp. What's happened to these people who used to be so gay, so they say, who once were called the wittiest in the world, who now are peevish, morose, and prudish? What's happened to them? Down here they haven't yet caught that disease—may heaven spare them! They are nice: how restful! How delightful! If you knew you would be the same or at least you would be tempted to. I feel great. I help around the house; I am learning the local cuisine; to do one's own work is restful! Day of lasagna, day of gnocchi, day of abbacchio! And do I ever drink lots of Frascati, we are just above the district, the vines are all around us, still black, with green heads. I think the nightingale has already begun, I think I heard him in the night; but I'm always asleep before it's time for him, I may have dreamed him; one night I'll wait for him; I'll be patient. I will start by meditating under an olive tree. I'll take a book: the moon may be strong enough. I read St. Augustine and some Buddhist writings. That's how I feel, that's how I felt when Fabrizio came on the scene.

They'll say: that woman was ripe for adultery. I said it myself. It was obvious, you couldn't miss it. Oh yes, it's easy afterwards, to say it. But before, you could have cut open my heart and seen nothing.

That's how I heard the nightingale. The moon was full, at last. Maybe that's what he was waiting for.

I left several days later. It was expected of me. So I left. Life is simple. As Philippe says.

Okay let's talk about love. Let's just talk about it a little!

"Did you have a good trip?"

"Wonderful. The weather was beautiful. You can't imagine what weather they have there. You can't even picture it when you're here you're so drowned in soup. Listen, I left under a blue sky. Really blue. Then above Milan we began to see clouds. Just clouds. But then, by the time we got to Paris, I'll never forget it. There, below us, a basin of filth, thick, black, nauseating. Unbearable. Asphyxiating. I said to myself: it isn't possible that people actually live down there. But that's where we landed. In the soup. We literally plunged into it. You couldn't see a thing. Grayness. Nothing. I was terrified, I swear. I said to myself They'll never find the field."

"You know perfectly well they have radar."

"That's not the point! Of course I know they have radar! It was an animal fear: I didn't want to go in there! Instinct for self-preservation, probably. Once we landed, I saw it was possible to see after all; I could make out the hangars and that kind of idiotic glass structure, I got out of the plane, everything looked ordinary, as usual, people walked, lived, they didn't seem to be about to crack up— and I was just like them. Only now I know we're living in shit: I saw it with my own eyes from up there. I saw us. Now I see myself. I know that I am walking in shit. No doubt of it. It's no joke. It's proven. I won't forget it again. At every moment I'll be aware of it."

"It's not necessary to cultivate obsessions."

Obsession: being aware of something real. (Note for the Célino-Philippian dictionary.) Function of the word: to make the real thing, which is troublesome, disappear into an imaginary one so that the party can go on. Another example: Atomic Bomb: paranoid obsession of certain sad souls from 1945 to . . . Function: to suppress the bomb. "Malta does not exist." That dictionary will really be cute. In fact, Célino-Philippian is too restrictive a title for such an important work. It should be more general. It's of public interest. I'll call it the Semantic Dictionary. Dammit, I'm really going to do it! Neo-Bourgeois Semantic Dictionary.

"You seem to have come back from your little trip in good spirits. You've found your tongue."

"Yes. It did me good."

Such is the way of the adulterous woman: she eats, she wipes her mouth, and then she says: it did me good.

What of it: it's true. Philippe even profits by it, I'm nicer. Influenced maybe by their customs down there, not yet readapted to those here. As for in bed, it's going better than before. So, it wasn't quite as perfect as all that?

There are three things outside my reach. And four which I cannot grasp: the flight of an eagle in the sky; the path of a serpent on the rock; the trace of a ship on the sea; and the mark of a man on a woman.

I don't understand either.

Suddenly I burst into tears at the table.

"What's the matter? What's come over you darling what is it?"

It was the full chorus from the Passion of St. John. The radio was presenting the entire work; I was listening almost without knowing I was when all of a sudden the full chorus burst on me. I wasn't expecting it. It fell on virgin soil, in all the weight of its beauty. So it took me by surprise and overwhelmed me.

"It's the music."

I could still love music, then. I was loving it again, it was given back to me. Happiness made me cry harder.

"The music?" Philippe looked at the machine which had caused this outburst. "Yes, of course, it's beautiful." He listens. "But all the same . . . You're sure that's all it is? There's nothing else, you're not hiding something from me?"

"Don't you think that's enough?"

"I don't know. . . . But it's an awfully violent reaction. . . . But then you're hypersensitive. I'm not sure it was the right thing for you to stop taking your medicine."

"Medicine for music?"

Thank God the chorus is over. I couldn't have gone on bearing the two of them together, Philippe and Bach. I'll buy the record.

"Put it more simply. I'm sensitive. Thank God."

Hypersensitive: capable of receiving impressions. Opposite of hypersensitive: Normal. Feeling nothing at all. Example: buying a radio for two hundred twenty thousand francs, turning it on while one is eating and hearing nothing that comes out of it.

The Dictionary is coming along. I've bought the Larousse and Flaubert's Dictionnaire des Idées Reçus. One must lean on the Masters, however lightly. And the last-named has a good deal about bull slinging in it too; it's more useful to me than that semester in philology which

I thought I should take in a fit of conscience, and whose
main result was to inspire Philippe to one of his better
efforts, on the theme Here we go again and how on
earth do you plan to use that my poor child at your age too,
you who never even bothered with a degree in spite of
all your so-called learning. Which is true. Never mind.
Philology was no help. Why are people so absolutely de-
termined to lose themselves in detail, what form of genius
drives them to choose exactly those subjects which are
farthest from the essential, what strange aversion keeps
them from seeking true knowledge—it is a mystery to
me, the mystery of mankind. Only mathematicians are
audacious they are so far off, but as soon as you approach
the concrete there is only flight, stampede, the Great
Myopia. In a moment of wild delirium I even thought of
founding a chair; I brought it up to Philippe so as to get a
rise out of him, which is always fun. Subject: How Man
Thinks. Let it go. I gave up Philology, I don't give a
damn about it. Aha, I knew it. My Poor Child, you've
given this up too, etc., a familiar tune. And what are you
doing with all those papers, what's this new whim?

"I'm making a dictionary."

"You're crazy. Better go to bed."

What for?

Because at last I can no longer delude myself. The
mechanism still works, but, these evenings, at midnight,
in the conjugal bed, the inspiration is lacking. And, sometimes, "I'm tired."

Love. —A: for a woman; total dedication to domestic
life, with night service. B: for a man; being satisfied with
this.

Love: acceptance and contemplation of Another, as he is, with no requirement of love in return. That's for the Dictionary of the Absolute. I'm doing a dictionary of the absolute, says Stephanie.

And your schoolwork! everyone says; and Philippe: You're influencing that child in a disastrous way. She sees only through your eyes, she imitates you, she copies your words. You're going to ruin her completely.

"I know someone who beats me all hollow in the ruin department."

"Who?"

"You."

"Me? What does that mean? What do you mean by that? Make yourself clear."

"I'll make you a catalogue."

"A catalogue, a dictionary! Haha! You are completely off your rocker, my poor child! You really are."

"Boing!"

"What does that mean?"

"Example of ruin: you are completely off your rocker my poor child you really are. That will do nicely."

"If you were really sure you weren't off your rocker it would take more than my ill-chosen words to 'ruin' you. It just proves how unstable you are."

"Boing! Second example: sowing doubt."

"Look, if you're going to stop me at every word—it's paranoid!"

"Boing!"

"You're really crazy!"

"Boing!"

"That's enough!"

"You're the one who asked me to make myself clear. And please notice, those weren't carefully chosen examples, I just took what came along. You can do much better."

"I really don't know what's wrong with you these days. You're . . . You're . . ."

"I'm what? You're looking for a word that isn't destructive, aren't you? and you can't find one. I'm . . . I'm . . . I am what I am, if you want to know, and maybe that's just what you don't like? What I am?"

"Only condition of love: that the Other consents to be loved. It's hard."

"But don't think it's any easier for the Other."

"What do you mean?"

"I refuse to explain."

"Would it be dangerous?"

"Very much so."

"How lovely."

"Let's go out. Let's take a walk. It's a nice day. It's a crime to be indoors in such weather. Anyway I have a date."

"It's a good thing."

Philippe said to me: I wonder what is the matter with you these days, you must be under some influence. Have you been seeing your old friends? I don't want him racking his brains for nothing poor darling. I began seeing them.

Thomas is starting a night club. It's fixed up like a real saloon, not too shoddy, but a bit like a whorehouse. You even wonder where the staircase in the back leads.

"Will there be a strip tease?" says Stephanie.

"Sure there'll be a strip tease."

"Will you hire Céline then?"

"Why Céline?"

"It wasn't true Stephanie I was kidding, I've never done strip tease. Publicly."

"But as a matter of fact you were quite gifted in private."

"How well I know," says Stephanie.

"How come?" says Thomas, who doesn't like to miss anything.

"She's making things up," I say.

"Yes, I'm making things up," says Stephanie.

"Well, well," says Thomas. "So, Céline, you changed much less than we thought!"

"I think I'm changing less all the time."

"Honestly?" he says, looking at me more closely. "Since when?"

"I don't want to think about it."

"Good God, the heartache you gave me! Do you want to know how I got over it? Sit down, what are you drinking? One evening, a long time afterwards, in a night club where I was doing some public relations work, I saw three couples come in, the kind that go to those miserable places. I was at the bar. I saw you, but you didn't see me. There was a stunning brunette with you."

"Julia," says Stephanie.

"She's dead," I say.

"What did she die of? So young."

"Of her husband. No, don't think he screwed her to death—oh no!—he was at the steering wheel."

"She deserved better. Anyway, I barely recognized you.

Don't be angry sweetie, you looked at least forty. You were . . . I can't tell you."

"Maybe it was what I wasn't?"

"It was painful to see—I mean for me—for other people you were just another woman, not bad at all, pretty, I'd say, prettier than you really are, really decked out, you know, in uniform. And looking like an ass. You. I said to myself, Oh my God, Céline! and I got over you. Sorry."

"It was only Madame Philippe Aignan."

"That's true I should have thought of that. Hello, Céline."

"Hello Thomas." And he kisses me.

No, seriously, I'm really fond of Thomas. I've always been fond of Thomas; he's a real man; he's a friend.

"But if you'll agree to strip—if my memory doesn't exaggerate—and if you've kept your shape—I'm ready to hire you. You don't just stumble on swinging girls who look good in their birthday suits—I'm hunting for them."

"The truth is Thomas I can't go around in my birthday suit; after all, I'm—married."

"How about me? I'd love to do a strip tease. I'm sure I have talent."

"I suppose I'd have standing room only from the second night on—"

"Sixteen years old," I say. "Not even that."

"But by the third I'd be in the clink, Lolita."

"Stephanie, if you please. Shit every time I move I send people to jail. It's paralyzing. Someday I'll make use of that characteristic to louse up someone that I don't like."

"Well it's too bad," says Thomas. "Between you you could have made up some damned good numbers. Because imagination is a rare quality, and to me, ordinary women who just take their clothes off in public for no reason are a bore."

"Are you looking for ideas? Maybe I could give you ideas without doing any more."

"That's not a bad thought. I'll buy that. Why shouldn't you work with me? I'm teamed up with a guy who's in the process of buying all the joints in Paris. I'd like to set up a little brain trust, public relations, some amusing people . . ."

I might be able to work. I might be able to work. Here is a new idea, dawning faintly, in the conditional.

I found him ten ideas for strips in a single afternoon. And better than the average, which I'm very familiar with, because this is one of the regular amusements of the Young Marrieds: we go to the strip joints. It's the Thing to Do. It's our little debauchery, with only calculated risks. Faithfully Ours, our Johns, with their gaze on a beautiful pair of unfamiliar tits. A way of being prudish while looking wicked. Above all, without consequences. In short, I'm in a position to make comparisons.

Stephanie made some up too, one of them for a girl of eleven, entitled: How to Send a Sucker to Jail.

But the price we paid was heavy.

"I have another idea," she says, "but maybe not for public consumption. Phaidros, a little girl of fifteen, would love Socrates, a young man. Socrates wouldn't have to do a thing, just let Phaidros do as she pleased . . ."

"Shall we take a walk?"

"No, I'm sick of that! My feet are beginning to hurt from all the walking! Céline, I rebel. You don't play fair. Because, my dear Socrates, I'd like to know where it says that being beloved only means being loved from afar?"

"You refuse to go for a walk?"

"Yes."

"For the third time."

"I refuse to go for a walk, Céline."

That was the price.

Thomas bought my ten ideas, and Stephanie's too, I'll have it done by a girl pretending to be younger than her age that'll have a certain charm. I took the check, which wasn't huge, but not to be sneezed at either, and which, at my request, was made out to Céline Rodes, and went to the bank to open an account under that name. But when they looked at my identification they asked me about the name Aignan. I said it was my husband's name. They told me that if I was married it made a difference, I'd have to have marital authorization.

I said I'd go get it. Then I went in another bank, showed my old papers, and opened an account. I hadn't known we were living under Napoleon. For my address, I gave Thomas', I went there quite often. At five Madame goes out.

In fact Thomas and I are working, most of the time. I have lots of ideas for his floor show: real Western numbers; target shooting with air pistols between the acts, and as a prize the right to drink with Way Mest, the star, an enormous adorable blonde with a throaty voice. And a lot of other things, they just pour out of me, my brain is a wellspring. When I have a little more time I'll act as his agent too; he'll pay me by the month.

When will I have a little more time?

"Céline, I want to open some charge accounts for you. I would like you to buy several dresses, really good ones. Price no object. It seems to me you've been letting your clothes go lately; besides, that isn't the only thing, but never mind it's all right that you hired a cleaning woman to help Juana it's natural but what isn't natural is that the results shouldn't at least be an improvement, you probably don't keep an eye on them, you're out all the time, I don't know what you're up to, besides, nor whom you see, but all right, that isn't what I want to talk to you about. I'd like to have you dress up a little. Go see the collections."

"It bores the hell out of me, you obviously don't know what it's like."

"All right, don't go," he says, without fussing, "but buy some suitable dresses. And can't you go to a good hairdresser? that hair of yours that's never grown out, I've finally accepted—you wore me down, but at least have it done. There are hairdressers who do miracles with four hairs. Ask Elizabeth where she goes."

"I know. You wait three hours there. That drives me crazy."

"It seems to me you have very little time to spare. At least for me."

167

"I'd like to have a job."

"What for? We have plenty of money, I don't need to have my wife work! And then what would you do? I can't imagine you in an office, they'd fire you at the end of a week, what is this sudden whim! It's time, I should be getting used to it. It's just one more of your things. I ought to know better than to worry about it. In any case it's out of the question even as a whim. I'm going to need you myself. I have a project under way."

"What?"

"I'll tell you when the moment comes. It's not yet ripe. All I ask of you now is to do as I tell you. It's a favor I'm asking, the least you can do is grant it, it seems to me."

"The least you can do." In exchange for all I, etc. These characters are always bargaining. Well since nothing is for nothing: you get what you pay for:

"But Philippe of course I'll be glad to, but you don't seem to realize how much time it takes to do even the smallest errand in Paris. . . . You reproach me for being out all the time, but once one is out, it's sometimes hard to get home again! You don't notice because you have a car . . ."

It worked. It wasn't difficult. Their system of barter is very costly. I got an Italian model.

But it's sad, really. It makes me melancholy, all that. Let's have a drink.

"I caught you at it, Céline! In flagrante delicto, perverting my little sister. I've heard them talking about it at home, but I didn't know how far it had gone. Now I see," says Bruno.

What he sees is Stephanie drinking a Coke while I have an anisette on the terrace of the Flore.

"What do they say at home?"

"Oh, nothing openly. They cover everything up. But they worry. You know how they are: concerned about our souls. Stephanie's must be in great danger. Someone discovered a secret diary . . ."

"That's not true I don't keep one! I'm not that dumb!"

"It was a shot in the dark. And Céline is going straight to hell. They loved you for a while, dear sister-in-law, but then . . ."

"I know, I hear the news, Philippe tells me every day. He doesn't know what's the matter with me."

"Anyway, your stock is going lower every hour with them, which means it's rising every hour for me. I was waiting for the chance to tell you, Céline; there it is. May I sit down?"

"I thought you already had."

"But I'm well brought up. I'll have an anisette too. Céline, at the beginning you dazzled me . . ."

"And I've been waiting for a chance to congratulate you on your quick-wittedness that day. But I haven't had one, we never see you Bruno."

"You disappointed me."

"I was doing my job."

"To Carmel, to Carmel! God that was funny! I felt wonderful. Reassured. Because for a long, long time I had cherished a dream," he says. "Do you know what it was?"

I said I didn't know.

"To see Big Brother cuckolded. . . . Didn't I catch a

look between you two? A knowing look? Do I understand you rightly? He is? If that's the case, I'll get an even bigger kick out of his becoming a deputy. All deputies should be cuckolds."

So that's what it was all about. Projects. Dresses. Munificence. Obviously nothing could be too fine for such a high enterprise. I ran to Balenciaga.

The next day we went to Dior. Et cetera. Nearly falling off the salon chairs from laughter, Bruno and Stephanie arbitrated: they were educating the deputy's wife. This monument would cost Philippe dear, but after all it was an investment, he would be repaid.

"Well, here you are at last. I was beginning to worry."

"I had to wait three hours for this dress to be ready," I say; it's about a third true, the rest of the time was spent on amusements. A marvelous dress, a dinner dress, four hundred thousand. "Good, this is the night to wear it," he says.

We were asked to an impromptu dinner—or else our invitation was obtained at the last moment by some trick. A formal dinner (shit) very important says Philippe, and so now I must know about (it's the moment it's the hour) his celebrated and up to now secret Great Projects, which may be mentioned at the table because now it was done it was Official (what a lather he's in), and to which I must be prepared to react in my appointed function for our Common Interests, take a breath. Because if things go the way he expects them to they can go very far, and I must prepare myself for a position to which a person of my kind is not often called, and to which his rise may elevate me. Inside his transparent skull I could see the hopes jostling each other, he saw himself as minister already, president of the Republic even, I was beside him cutting ribbons and breaking bottles of champagne on aircraft carriers. What a life. Finally out of all this mountain he gave birth to his mouse and sat back to consider the effect. I asked what ticket he's running on. He seemed surprised at the question, which led us to such ridiculous side issues. He named the majority party of the moment.

"I thought you were a radical?"

Decidedly I was showing a sordid interest in trivial detail. Nevertheless he condescended to explain:

"They were all right for a while. But they have become very unrealistic; they have adopted outrageous positions; there's no hope for them. Anyway, all that isn't important, hurry up and get dressed. Let's see that dress. Really it's very nice. It will do."

"Four hundred thousand. But you are a realist, of course?"

"What? Try to understand Céline that if you want to get something done it's better to be in office than out. Are you getting dressed?"

"That depends on what you want to get done."

"What?"

"If it's some kind of dirty work it's better to be out. If you have any moral principles."

"Listen Céline hurry up instead of talking so much, I don't want to be late to this dinner."

He obviously isn't sure there's a place card for him, it's

all happened so quickly, and at the last moment, he wants to be there to make sure it's arranged. . . .

"At least there's one vote you won't get. Mine."

"What?"

Now he is openly surprised. He stops in the middle of tying his tie. I was the minister's wife, I was cutting ribbons, he was addressing the crowds, and now what's all this nonsense about votes?

"All right, you can use your vote for a curl paper if you like. In any case I'm not a candidate in the district where you vote—since it seems you do vote. If you call it voting to exhibit your family skeletons at the polls."

"Look, Philippe, it's just that I don't vote for that party."

"Madame places her political ideas above her emotions. Madame does not kowtow to her husband."

"Philippe, don't mix metaphors. Either you exhibit skeletons or you place ideas . . . oh what am I bothering for it's hopeless your brain works that way."

"My brain works just fine, thank you."

"Absolutely fine. It's a perfect bourgeois brain. A real model of its kind. In the last analysis I'm really grateful to have had a chance to examine it closely. In the last analysis there is no such thing as a waste of time."

"I can't even stop to think about all the outrages you manage to perpetrate because . . ."

"Because you'll be late for this dinner which is more important than they are."

"Precisely. I have other things to think about right now. I'll just say that it's a real pleasure for a man to know his wife is behind him; and that it really makes it worth while to knock myself out giving you an easy and glamorous life for which you have no appreciation whatsoever," he says with a large gesture to indicate my appearance, Balenciaga real pearls elegant coiffure, which he forgets (or pretends to) is only decked out this way on his orders and if it were up to me . . .

"Are you doing all this for me? Dear Philippe!"

"You're the one who profits by it, as I just told you! Verbally, you spit on 'bourgeois brains,' but you don't spit on the results of them! At least have enough dignity to keep your mouth shut!"

"One last word, though: I must tell you that I won't be the wife of a deputy on that ticket. It's a question of honor. I want to give you fair warning."

"Big talk. What do you imagine? That that matters? Listen Céline, you are free to think what you please—if you think—but allow me the same freedom. Since you consider yourself 'a democrat.' I do what I want, and all I ask of you is not to get in my way, and among other things at the moment to go to this dinner with me and behave yourself so as not to interfere with my projects. I hope that much is understood."

It was. I proved it by trotting out all the charm at my disposal for the benefit of the personages Philippe pointed out to me as important to his career. He left that party with four invitations for other dinners—and be sure to bring your adorable wife—and convinced that the harsh words exchanged before we left home had gone where all words go, into oblivion. In high good humor was Philippe, and enchanted with me to the point of letting me see it. He kissed me!

"You see what I can do when I put my mind to it. Maybe the dress helped, it's wildly sexy, that's the only way to get such results, it's pretty expensive but it's money well spent. And I have three dates with men for next week."

"What?" he said startled and passing a red light. I took out my engagement book and showed him the names, the dates and the places, which I had carefully noted. And no small-timers: only the most useful ones.

"You're mad! I didn't ask you to go that far!"

"I didn't go they came."

"But—what are you going to do?"

"I'll do whatever you want Philippe. If you tell me to go I'll go, if you tell me not to I won't."

"But Céline . . . are you blind . . . or did you do it on purpose . . . you put me in a position . . ."

Shitty, eh? Tralala. I'm having a ball, in my little corner. You sent your wife out whoring with four hundred thousand francs on her ass and afterwards you want everything to be neat and proper and called something different. Now he has it right back in the kisser.

In fact I behaved very nicely. I didn't go after these schnooks, not even for Philippe's reputation. I played hard to get. They beg me. They call me on the telephone. I suggest their ringing up at times when Philippe is almost bound to be at home. That way he can hear what's going on. Everything out in the open. Afterwards when he's off canvassing the hinterlands, cradle of the family, where he's being introduced, he gets the jitters about it.

He's quite wrong. That kind of trash is not my cup of tea. If it were up to me I wouldn't go near them with a

ten-foot pole. No when Philippe is away I use the time for
work; I pass my evenings in my saloon, watching the public's reaction to my ideas; trying to improve them and to
find new ones, I play hostess, I help Thomas, who has
also hired a very good pianist, very funny, a big drinker
and a real music lover, with whom I can talk; Nicolas and
I went to choose a recording of the Passion according to
St. John together.

As soon as you leave the bourgeois world, you begin to
catch a glimpse of men again.

"I come home and the house is empty. I don't know
where to find you. The maid is out. I wait. At dinner-
time you still aren't there. Nor the maid either. I have to
eat at my parents' house!" he sputters, overcome with
indignation.

"If you want things to be ready for you, let someone
know you're coming back. There's a telephone here. I
was expecting you tomorrow."

"Let someone know I'm coming back to my own
house! That would really be the end!"

"But if you want everything ready for you—"

"Besides, I did telephone. No one home. And I have to
wait until three in the morning before I finally see you!
to know whether you're alive! Where were you?"

"I was out."

"A rather feeble explanation. I notice you don't say
with whom."

"With your brother."

It was true, too.

"Now it's my brother. First my sister, then my brother. And you laugh!"

"But it's funny Philippe!"

"Oh sure, you think it's funny! The house is empty, my wife is out God knows where, and besides it isn't much different when I'm home, Madame has her little excursions, her own friends—and her spiritual activities!"

A pile of leaves fly up from my table, swept by his hand. My papers! He's been prying into my papers!

"You've been prying into my papers!"

"What of it? Have you secrets?"

"You, you bourgeois! polite on the outside but underneath the lowest of the low! You are all sickening!"

I bend down to pick up the pages. I try to put them in order. I make myself be calm. Anyway I'm not really angry. I'm in a strange state. Something is happening.

"Oh, they're well worth stooping for," he says from on high, always the gentleman standing tall with all his six feet one inch, blond, gray eyes, medium nose, medium mouth, slightly puffy chin. "Oh, they're worth it! What talent, what genius! I didn't know I was living with a prodigy, haha! metaphysics and strip tease! My poor girl! I advise you to submit them to the kind of publisher who specializes in case histories. That's where you'd go over big."

A tear falls on the Dictionary. I wait. No more follow. It must be the last. I see Philippe's feet in front of me. I smile at them.

"Knock it off Philippe Aignan it doesn't work any more. The only thing that bothers me this time is your indiscretion."

"What do you expect, my dear, when I find myself alone in the house, in My Own house . . ."

It's funny, they don't realize when things are really serious. They go on yammering.

". . . while I wait, with nothing to do, with hours going by . . . I have to find something to do . . . I was tempted. . . . I asked myself where my wife was. . . . I asked myself the fatal question of who my wife was . . . this stranger . . . in my house."

"Had you never asked yourself before?"

"Look Céline will you tell me? What is the matter with you? What is happening to you? I don't know you any more, what has been the matter with you lately?"

"I'm alive."

"You're what?"

"I'm alive Philippe that's all. And that's what upsets you."

"Certainly, since your life is apart from me!"

"But my dear love, that's just it: with you, I die!"

WHAT THERE IS and what's good in a Carmel is God. God, at least, is perfect. That's His definition. And, from the moment one accepts Him, one surrenders oneself without fear, it can only be to something higher. As high and no higher than one's definition of perfection permits, but still, to something higher. Whereas if one surrenders oneself to a Creature, where does it lead?

Profane love is shit.

"But Céline . . ."

"All right, I didn't say it very well. I'm still in shock. But it's true."

"But still, Céline, when I love you . . ."

"Stephanie I hope you don't love me, I hope you love through me."

"What through you?"

"We don't know what. And it's much better like that. Maybe, someday, we'll know. We live in that hope."

My dear Philippe,

You invited me to Carmel. I followed you. I put myself in your care. I placed great trust in you. And that was very rash. I'm afraid my dear Philippe that you had mistaken yourself for Another. Having surrendered myself to you I sank downward. One man does not make a Carmel. So imagine, a deputy! . . . As I warned you, I will not be the wife of a deputy on that ticket for even an hour.

You have been elected, I congratulate you, and I'm leaving you.

Since I can't see that you'll suffer from the loss of a person about whom you like nothing except her defeats, I leave this house in all serenity, sure that I'm causing no tears. Anyway your success will make up for everything. And I have no regrets for myself either: I didn't waste my time; thanks to you, by the fortunes of love, I've been able to get a close look at that Machine of which you are at once an unconscious gear and a conscious operator, and which is, for those of us who are still breathing, an instrument of mortality. It was worth getting to know, worth seeing how it works, in order to learn to defend myself from it and so save my life. Thanks for being that opportunity, Philippe, I don't know why I loved you, but it wasn't in vain, you gave me keys which I'll know how to use. Thank you.

For practical matters. Maître Martineau will get in touch with you. I think your code demands that in divorce proceedings a man in your position should blame himself in order to preserve the honor which is indispensable to his career, and particularly to that one on which you've embarked; so, although all the faults are mine, I'm quite willing to give you that privilege. However if your irritation overcomes your self-interest, I would be ready to agree, political disagreements not being grounds for divorce under the Napoleonic Code, to produce whatever is legally necessary in abundance.

I have taken a few personal possessions which I believe I have earned. In return I leave you the dresses intended for the deputy's wife—I won't have any use for them, they may come in handy.

Céline Rodes

P.S. Your dinner is ready.

"Where will you leave it?"

"In the fridge. That's where they always look first."

"I can see it now," says Bruno. "*The Candidate's Return*, by Courbet. Clothed in glory and in heartache. Smiling at his voters and weeping on his hearth."

"Heartache? You don't know him! The only thing Philippe will say is: The Whore!"

"Well, shall I take the suitcases?" says Bruno. "No last regrets?"

They told me, all those timid, frightened souls: think it over, have you thought it over, are you sure, are you very sure that you aren't making a mistake, you're going to be all alone again, and in your old age . . . and if you get sick . . . and if . . . and if. They told me There are crises in all marriages everybody knows it, the three-year crisis, the five-year crisis, the ten-year crisis, the twenty-five-year, the forty-year, one gets over them, time takes care of it. I'm sure time takes care of it that's the worst thing. But I ask them were yours over political differences? That's the whole question.

"My God this was an ugly apartment! And I am the author of this abortion! What was the matter with me?"

"You were in love."

"That can't be it. It must have been something else. It must have another name. What? I'm going to find one. Come on whatever happens I have to go and vote."

"And if he isn't elected?"

"Bah. I'm not going to unpack my suitcases, it's too much trouble."

"Céline . . ." says Bruno.

"Is it too heavy?"

"No, it's light."

"I took as little as possible."

"That wasn't what I meant."

Five flights. One less than before, my old room wasn't free. Here's the door. I look at it. One never knows what one will find behind a door.

"Céline," says Bruno sitting on the suitcases, "do you know what's happening to me?"

"You're getting tired."

"No, I'm in love."

"My God!" groans Stephanie, and sits down too.

"It never hurts to sit down and think things over awhile," I say, doing the same. "Whatever they are."

"Let's think," says Bruno.

"We have plenty of time," I say.

"I love life," says Stephanie.

"We have plenty of time."

Tomorrow, the day after, eternity. But now my friends

182

you are going to leave me. To leave me. To leave me to enter my own house. One never knows what one will find behind a door.

I close it behind me. I lean against it. Here I am. I look around.

I breathe.

At last. Alone.